WANTIN

Truth Devour

Published in 2013
by Truth Devour

Interior layout and design
by Publicious Pty Ltd
www.publicious.com.au

Book cover design by:
Brightpixel Design
www.brightpixeldesign.com.au

Catalogue-in-Publication details available
from the National Library of Australia

ISBN: 978-0-9922999-0-3

Also available in ebook
ebook ISBN: 978-0-9922999-1-0

To be yourself in a world that is constantly trying to make you something else is the greatest accomplishment.

Ralph Waldo Emerson

Intensity

He watches me as I enter the room. No words are spoken, just an exchange of glances that make the little hairs on the back of my neck stand on end. I am not sure how long he has been here waiting for me to arrive but I can see that he is intent on not wasting any time. Slowly he walks towards me. His hands glide across my neckline, reaching towards my back. In one swift move he has unclasped the clip that releases my halter-neck dress from my body. It gently falls to the floor, caressing my curves on the way down.

Without skipping a beat, he slowly walks around me as if to inspect the package presented before him. My skin feels electrified with the anticipation of what is to come. The simple extension of his touch has been known to send my senses into overdrive. I have no idea why he has this ability to make me shiver with delight. It is disconcerting that my body is so willing to surrender itself to him.

He stands behind me, close enough for me to detect his warmth but there is no contact. Patiently he waits for his moment and then reaches around towards the centre of my abdomen, lightly skipping the surface of my skin with random fingers on his right hand. He traces from my midriff to my waist, down to my buttock and then slowly back again. I gasp at the sensation and close my eyes to heighten the sense of our connection.

In this moment he knows he has all the power because I am willing to surrender myself to him. I want him. As he faces me he waits for my eyes to open. His right thumb traces the outline of my lips while his left hand caresses the back of my neck. He smiles and kisses me passionately. I moan as I release the tension of the day into his mouth and greet his tongue with mine. He is an incredible kisser.

I take his hand and lead him towards the bed. He smiles as I start to undress him. He knows that I am not as patient. I want to rip his clothes off and have my wicked way but this time I am taking my time. I slowly unbutton his shirt while staring into his eyes. I am certain he thinks that I will cave at any moment and pounce but he is mistaken. Tonight it is my turn to make him yearn. I want his body to ache as he has made mine so that he can appreciate the vulnerable position that I allow myself to be in.

As I reach across his shoulders I pull his shirt down and entrap his arms in the sleeves. I gently kiss his neck then head towards his chest. I softly kiss him down his midriff until I reach his belly button. I take some of his fine little hairs in my mouth, gently tugging. He stares down at me with intense concentration. I'm feeling quietly triumphant.

On my knees, I run my hands along the outline of his visible erection. The clasp from the zipper on his jeans is now firmly between my teeth. I smile at him as I ever so slowly unzip him. I ease his jeans down, pry his legs apart and run my fingers from his ankle to his inner thigh, brushing the outline of his scrotum and back down the other thigh to his ankle. He closes his eyes, puts his head back and groans.

It is at this moment that I feel inspired. I stand and head towards the kitchen.

"I'm a little thirsty. Would you like me to bring you back a drink?"

He focuses on my wicked smile. "Oh, no, you don't!" He frees his arms from the shackles of his shirt, fumbles to release his feet from his jeans and runs towards me.

I screech and giggle as he sweeps me into his arms. He takes me across to the bed, throws me on it. In one swift carnal move he rips off my panties and is positioned between my legs. He pauses to look at me panting and then lunges forward to kiss me with the intent of an impaler.

Rhythmically intertwined, we synchronise our gyrations. My legs are wrapped around him so he cannot escape. I groan as he plunges deep inside me. I am wet and swollen from the buildup of our mutual torment. I want to make this last but the intensity overwhelms me. He can see that I am on the edge and defiantly quickens the pace. My body shudders with the sweet release that can only be achieved by such moments of bliss. He too climaxes and falls on top of me, panting.

Haiti

I was six years old and my world was insular in experience. My parents were avid travellers who spent months and at times years in different countries living within a chosen culture. I would like to tell you that they did this for some esoteric or spiritual reason, but in truth it was simply because they could and, more importantly, they wanted to. They had no financial concerns and decided way before I was a happy accident that they would roam the world and see what was on offer. I knew no different at the time so I never thought to mind that there was nowhere to call home.

My fondest memories were linked to where we were based in Port-au-Prince. The Haitians had an amazing sense of community and pride. I am not sure whether it was because I was a child, but I felt welcome there surrounded by nurturing souls. Everyone smiled, joy filled the warm musty air and I was enveloped in a metaphoric cocoon created by their care. It was in this place among these people that I would experience my first love and would encounter strange events that in retrospect were the practice of Vodou.

"Com, Miss, you will be late for school," said my nanny.

With a scowl on my face and a stomp of my foot, I yelled, "I don't want to go." I sat on the floor with my hands covering my eyes, hoping that my defiance would be accepted and I could stay home.

"Com, Miss, you will be late for school," she insisted.

Marlee was a middle-aged lady who my parents had hired to be my makeshift nanny while they explored the island. She had the biggest smile and the loudest laugh I had ever heard. When I had first met her I was terrified because her two front teeth were missing, so when she screeched with laughter I could see this gaping hole into the darkness. Trust me, at that time in my mind's eye it was scarier than I can describe.

Looking through the car window as we arrived at the union school, I was daunted by the size of the facility. I had never been to school before and because of my parents' insistence on travelling I never really had any friends my age. I was out of my comfort zone and none too pleased about it.

The Union School was a private facility that catered for all nationalities. When Marlee took me into my kinda class room I was overwhelmed by the sight of the kids running around. A random mixture of laughter, screeching and crying filled the air.

Marlee pushed me gently into the centre of the room. "All good now, Missy, go on now."

I was hesitant, to say the least, and didn't know what I was doing there. In shock, I stood watching the mash of events, too distracted to notice that Marlee's hand was no longer on my back and that indeed she had left me there to fend for myself.

"Hush, hush, to your seats, please," called out the lanky fellow who had walked into the room. He greeted my eyes with a smile that revealed big yellow teeth.

"Well, hello. My name is Mr Laylor. What is your name, young lady?"

I stared at him and recoiled as he reached his arm out to place it on my shoulder.

He bent down to greet me at my eye level and said, "It's okay. I know that this all seems a little scary. I promise you that this is a place of fun. That is what we are here for today, right, children? To have fun."

The kids, who were all sitting down now, yelled out their approval. I was horrified to be left standing in front of them all.

I looked back at Mr Laylor. He was about to speak when I heard a male voice come from my right.

"Hello, my name is Bodhi."

I turned to look at the newcomer and whispered a barely audible, "Hi."

"What's your name?"

"Talia," I responded, staring at my feet.

"You can sit next to me if you like, Talia." He reached out and took my hand and walked towards the chairs.

"Wonderful! WONDERFUL!" Mr Laylor said with a clap of his hands and a beaming smile.

Bodhi pointed to a chair and I sat while he, without another glance, sat in the seat beside me. I clasped my hands together and stared at my shoes.

***

One day melted into the next at the Union School. I became accustomed to the routine, the games we played and indeed the chance to see Bodhi. He was a light-framed boy with fine dirty-blond hair and the most piercing blue eyes I had ever seen. He seemed to watch out for me and he always chose me as his partner in the paired games, even if I wasn't very good. We never really spoke that much to one another, but regardless, he was always by my side. I liked that about him.

Bodhi and I spent time together after school playing games. Marlee made us some dinner and then we walked Bodhi home. She always had this smirk on her face when it was time for us to say goodbye. We both stood there, looking at each other and then eventually one of us would say, "See ya," and head off.

Marlee giggled on the way home, referring to the perfection of young love. At the time, I had no idea what she was talking about. I mostly ignored her when she started to babble about it.

Six months flew by; my parents were still travelling from place to place, dropping past to tell me about their adventures. I didn't mind that they weren't around. I had my routine; I was settled and felt happy. It was only when Bodhi told me that his parents were heading back to the United States that I started to feel unsettled. It never dawned on me that the relationships I was forging in this school were destined to end. All the children had parents like mine, who were in the country for only a short time.

The news upset me greatly. I couldn't sleep, I lost my appetite and was sad. Marlee watched over me while I went through a new suite of emotions that I was not to understand until I was older. All I wanted to do was cry. I skipped school for a few days because I could not bear to have my emotions betray me and burst into tears in front of Bodhi.

"Talia, you have a visitor." Marlee poked her head round the door to my bedroom and gestured for me to come out.

I shook my head and turned away. I heard whispers and then footsteps leading into my room and up to my bed.

"Talia." Bodhi reached out to touch my shoulder.

"Com on, Talia, please say something."

He sat on the edge of my bed and played with my hair. I took a deep breath, turned so I was next to him. For the longest while we sat there in silence while I stared at his hands.

Bodhi reached out towards my chin and gently lifted my face so that my eyes greeted his. He smiled as he leant in to kiss a rolling tear. "Salty," he said.

We both laughed.

"I don't want you to go."

"I don't want to go but I have to. My mom and dad are heading home and I have to go too."

"I know, but it's not fair. I only just found you."

"If we did it once, we can do it again," Bodhi said with an air of certainty and a confident nod.

Marlee had organised a little party for Bodhi and me in celebration of our friendship and to wish him farewell on his journey. My parents were away on another of their trips so it was just the three of us. She had made the most amazing cake with turquoise and orange frosting. It was garish but vibrant to look at and delicious to eat. Marlee spent the evening telling us stories of powerful friendships forged by fate and the need to sustain the balance of love.

Bodhi and I were high on sugar, paying no attention as she lit the room with candles and plaited our hair together in two finely intertwined patterns. A bowl of flaming herbs released a musty smell as it exhaled a steady stream of smoke. The storytelling had ceased. Marlee muttered words I couldn't understand. Her hands waved in the drifting smoke, making it dance in swirls above our heads. I reached out and held Bodhi's hand, squeezing it tightly as an emotional intensity built up inside me.

"I never want to let you go," I blurted out to him.

"I will find you, I promise," he said assuredly.

I looked into his piercing blue eyes and believed him. I knew in that moment that we would indeed find one another again.

Marlee snapped with the scissors. Swiftly, using a turquoise and orange ribbon to bind the ends of the plaits, she placed them before us. Her eyes were dull, seemingly lost in thought.

In an unfamiliar, deep, resonating voice, she said, "Each take one and put them in a safe place. If you want to in this lifetime, you are bound to find one another now." She walked out of the room and left us alone.

I remember the silence, the musty smell of the incense that surrounded us and the look in Bodhi's eyes that confirmed a promise that one day we would meet again.

Surrender

It had been six weeks since Bodhi and his family had left for home. School was no longer the same. In fact, anything that we had shared together no longer seemed to hold any joy. I had this dull ache inside me that I could not appease. I was longing for my parents to come back so that I could beg them to follow. This had been their longest stint away from me that I could recall.

Marlee was my saving grace. She now became my constant. She seemed to place no effort in looking after me. It was as though she enjoyed doing it. I loved her for that.

There are some moments in life, no matter how old you are; you never forget them. I was sitting on the front porch drinking some freshly squeezed lemon water that Marlee had made for me when a weather-beaten car pulled up. Two men climbed out and came to the porch. I didn't move and returned the stare of the man with the yellow eyes. He seemed to find it amusing.

"You are going to be a heart-breaker when you grow up, little one," he said as a smile landscaped across the horizon of his mouth to reveal surprisingly perfect white teeth. "Where is your nanny?"

I didn't respond. I continued to look at him and then glanced at the other fellow standing behind him. He seemed distant. He may have been present but he was not really there. I felt as though he were lost. Perhaps it was my own state of awareness that made me attuned to the energy that he was projecting. Maybe I was reading my own pain, using him as a mirror to externalise my grief over missing Bodhi.

Marlee came to the door. Her eyes widened, her lips tightened and then she glanced at me.

"Come in." She gestured and the two strangers walked inside.

I could hear muffled voices but could not make out what they were saying. The walls were thin as paper so they must have been keeping quiet intentionally.

***

Later that same morning, Marlee decided that she was going to take me for a day trip to her village to meet her family. We travelled in the car with the top down for what seemed like hours. There was diversity to the changing landscape that was visually pleasing. I played games with the shadows of the dappled sunlight that danced on my face. The air was cooler in the shade of the canopy of trees. The blurred screeching of insects melted into one as we travelled towards her village. I had never been outside of Port-au-Prince, so my senses were delighted with the new stimulus.

Marlee sang along to the crackling radio. The static drove me mad but she didn't seem to notice. We turned down a road and headed along a bumpy dirt track. The dust that rose behind us in a wafting cloud warned of our presence. I could see smoke streaming up between the trees ahead so I knew that we had to be close. An unfamiliar, overwhelming sweet smell hung in the air.

Crowds of people waited in the clearing beside a bevy of small colourfully painted concrete houses. Their faces shone with happiness at our arrival. The villagers quickly surrounded Marlee. They were all eager to hug and kiss her. She, in return, cried and smiled, hugging and kissing them all frantically. She squealed when she picked up the children, who were all trying to clamber into her arms. This was my first witness of community affection.

Marlee introduced me to her mother, her five sisters and four brothers, not to mention a flurry of other people who merged into a blurred tapestry of happiness. I had never realised that she had such a big family. In truth, I had never even considered that Marlee belonged somewhere.

Watching them together was surreal. In the presence of her family and community I could see aspects of her I had not seen before. A daughter, a sister, a friend …

They had planned a big party in honour of Marlee's return and people scurried around to organise the grounds for the evening celebrations. They threw a stack of wood into a worn fire pit. Stones were wedged together and bound by a strange black thick and shiny tar-like substance to create a small wall to act as a firebreak. There was no order to the way people placed the twigs. The only aim seemed to be to build the stack higher and higher and in that they were most successful.

They placed tables and chairs on the outskirts of the area. A band with makeshift instruments set themselves upwind of the smoke. One of the men caught my interest. He had several forty-four-gallon drums cut to different heights and he had wrapped a cloth around two solid tree branches that he used to hit the drums, whacking them, moving them from one direction to the next in search of the perfect sound. He was fascinating to watch. His arms were thin but muscular. Once he was satisfied with the positioning, he proceeded to create a series of beats that were rhythmical and hypnotic to my ears.

The sickly sweet smell that I had noticed when I first arrived had reappeared. It was a fusion of smells: burnt molasses, banana, vanilla and something that I could not identify. People started to appear, as though the beat of the drum had summoned them. The women wore colourful clothing and had lovely big flowers in their pinned-up hair. The men wore white. Bright, crisp, perfect white. No-one wore shoes. They passed an open jug from one to another, drinking and laughing. The boar that had been killed earlier in the day was now cooking over a fire in an outdoor kitchen. All the food to be shared was set out on a large table. It was impressive to see all these people joined together to celebrate Marlee's homecoming.

Where is she? I wondered.

I been so consumed by my new surroundings that I had not realised that we had been separated since our arrival. It was unlike her to leave me unattended for so long. Perhaps in the safety of her community she felt I didn't need minding. Still, I could feel a growing sense of being alone. In amongst a sea of laughter and warm smiling faces, I was very much on my own.

As the sun drew a curtain across the evening sky the music grew louder and the villagers drunker. I noticed that women were the only ones dancing around the bonfire. Their movements were random. Marlee's sister-in-law leapt about; another lady was on her knees, gyrating and snarling. We all heard the same rhythmic beat, yet they each seemed to interpret it differently. The men gathered in groups, engulfed in their banter. They didn't seem to want to take stock of what their mothers, wives and daughters were doing. Instead they smoked, laughed and drank. Everyone knew his or her place and purpose.

In an instant the music stopped and everyone froze. The outline of a person dressed in a fantastical array of colours was coming towards us from the shadow of the houses. I am not sure why the villagers kept so still but instinctually I did the same. My pulse quickened and I could hear the sound of my heart beating. I wanted my mummy and daddy. As the figure closed in I realised it was Marlee. She looked beautiful. I had never seen her dressed up before. She stopped when she was in front of me; her eyes stared into the depths of the raging flames of the bonfire.

Bam, bam, bam! Three strokes of the drum. In complete synchronicity, everyone moved to stare into the fire. Words I could not understand were chanted. I looked up at Marlee and she stared down at me. She placed a hand on each of my arms, her fingers firmly wrapped around my biceps, drawing me closer to her.

In a deep unfamiliar voice she said, "It is time to dance with the dead. You must see. You must see."

She released my arms, stepped back and blew a powder into my face and rubbed it into my arms. It all happened so quickly that I had no chance to react. Warmth tingled across my body and a sense of fuzziness engulfed me. The chanting grew louder and the drums started again. It all happened so fast and yet I felt as though time had slowed down. My mind was clear but I could not speak. The pulsating resonance of the drums surrounded me in waves that beckoned my body to move. Yielding to its calling, I fell to my knees, reefing my body forwards and backwards, my fingers touching the dusty granules of dirt around me.

It felt like liquid and I could see ripples of water in waves around me. I sank deeper into the earth with each movement. I had no fear or inclination to stop. I wanted to be immersed in the rhythm of the music to the core of my being. The pace grew faster and faster; I sank deeper into the ground until I was under water. I could taste the salt on my lips.

Looking up, I could see what seemed to be the bottom of a small boat. The sun rippled through the water, creating a false barrier between where I was and where I felt I needed to be. As I glided across to where I felt drawn I could see the silhouette of two figures. The warmth that I had felt in the presence of the sunlit water was absent now. My skin was covered in goose bumps and I started to tremble. The closer I came to the objects the colder I became. Still I felt compelled to move forward. I needed to see. I wanted to see.

I was close enough to touch them now. They were entangled in some sort of ocean reeds. I removed the green strands and saw that the encased objects were human, rigid and cold to touch. I couldn't see their faces. I needed to see their faces. I kept trying to remove the reeds but they kept reappearing. My sense of urgency transformed to panic.

In frenzy, I clawed to free them.

Something started to pull them down deeper into the ocean. The same force was drawing me to the surface. I tried to fight and swim back towards them. I didn't want to leave. I wasn't ready to give up. I needed to see.

I needed to know. My tears merged with the salty water to form crystalised electric-blue droplets that floated with the current down towards them. My screams pleading for them to come back had no sound, yet the silence was deafening.

The crow of a rooster resonated in my eardrums. I opened my eyes, glanced around and realised that I was lying on a bed of straw in one of the homes. I looked across and there was Marlee sleeping nearby. Other bodies lay on the floor in the room too. They all seemed to be in a deep sleep. I lay watching the sun's rays unveil the dust particles dancing in the air. I could recall the experiences of the night before in every detail except for how I had got to bed.

A beautiful elder entered the room. She looked around at the still bodies, made eye contact with me and gestured for me to follow. I quietly rose and walked after her. When I turned the corner she was waiting for me at the outdoor kitchen area. She passed me a glass with some liquid in it and proceeded to cook. I studied the weathered features of her face. I'm not sure how old she was, but I could see that at one stage she would have been a stunning woman. She glanced at me in a fleeting moment, hinting at a smile and a nod, as though she could read my thoughts and agreed with my sentiments.

As the heat of the pan sizzled, my mind drifted back to the ocean and the two silhouettes I had seen. There was a familiarity to the moment that I could not place. I snapped out of the thought when a plate of warm food was placed in front of me. The elder was now sitting across from me, smiling, her arms folded.

In an inexplicable moment of need, I looked at her and said in a whisper, "My parents are dead, aren't they?"

She did not change her expression or the position of her body. She continued to stare at the plate she had placed before me as though waiting for me to eat. I picked up the utensil and gathered some of the food. It smelt good. I placed the first spoonful in my mouth and felt my stomach churn in anticipation. The elder let out a sigh of relief as she touched my left arm with her warm weathered hand. I looked into her eyes and could not see an end to her depth. There was a long pause as we gazed at one another.

She broke the silence with a single word. "Yes."

It wasn't long before the villagers stirred. They came across to the outdoor kitchen and served themselves breakfast. The elder left the table and stood near the back of the stove. Her eyes connected with mine in a way to provide reassurance. My head spun at the idea that my parents were dead. I knew it to be true.

Marlee came out and placed her hand on my shoulder. The elder smiled and left. I looked at Marlee and she stared back at me. She placed her hands on either side of my face and nodded.

"My mum and dad are dead," I whispered.

She lifted me from my chair and held me tight in her arms. Her warm breath lay like a blanket on my ear. "I know, my child. I know."

The villagers started to hum and gently sway from side to side. They all took turns in passing by us and touching my forehead. I felt betrayed by the tears streaming down my eyes. I was lost in the presence of these kind people and could not manage to appease the overwhelming depth of my impeding sorrow.

Reality

The remaining time spent at the village was a haze. When we arrived back at the house in Port-au-Prince the two men who had been there before were on the porch waiting for us. The air was still and the heat unbearable. Sweat dripped from the first man's brow as he fanned his face with his hat.

"We have been waiting a long time for you, Missy," he said, revealing his pearl-white teeth in a smile.

I squeezed Marlee's hand and she brought me in closer to her body. Marlee and the men once again went inside and spoke while I sat on the porch. Everything seemed sticky from the heat. Muffled voices spoke behind the thin fibro sheets of the house walls. I could understand some words but nothing that allowed me to string together what they were talking about.

When they finally headed out the door, the man looked at me and then at Marlee and said, "We will be back tomorrow."

He placed his hat on his head, ushered the other man forward and then proceeded to the car.

Inside, Marlee was busy in the kitchen organising a

vegetable stew. "You have to eat, Talia. You need your strength now."

I could see that she was concerned about something. The wrinkles on her brow glistened with sweat. She chopped at the vegetables with intent. As she increased her chopping motion the veggies started to fall off the edge of the board and roll onto the floor. She was frantic in her preparation and didn't seem to notice. It was a sign that we were running out of time. I didn't know what tomorrow was to bring but I knew that more change was imminent.

***

That evening after supper Marlee took me into the room that she called her place of prayer. She sat me down on the floor and asked me to look into the flames of the candles that were before me. I stared into the transient light. All the flames were perfectly still, except one. The flame pulsated and the tip morphed from flame to smoke that released into the air with a swirl. I was mesmerised.

Marlee walked around me clockwise, dropping a mixture of white powder and salt onto the floor in the shape of a circle. She chanted the words: truth, honesty, protect, serve – over and over. At times she called out names, none of which were familiar to me. The longer I stared at the flames the darker my surroundings appeared. Marlee's voice became a distant hum as I fell deeper into the candles' inviting flame.

***

In the morning I woke on the floor in the circle that surrounded me. The candles had burnt to a stub and were a coagulated pile of wax. My neck was stiff from my positioning and I could feel the cool breeze of the morning air between the cracks in the floorboards. I looked around the stark room and could see the smoke stains on the walls from the years of being subjected to burning candles. I reached out, took a blob of the melted wax and put it in my pocket before leaving the room.

Marlee was in the kitchen making breakfast. I could smell the fat from the meat and eggs that she was cooking. I went into the bathroom and had a shower to take the week's sweat and grime from my clogged pores. The cool water enveloped me and I suddenly broke down and cried. I curled up in the bath and let the water pelt on me as I wept. My parents were dead. I was alone.

Shortly after I reached the breakfast table, someone knocked on the door. I could hear the voices of a man and a woman. Marlee looked across at me, took a deep breath and left to answer. My heart beat louder and louder as the steps drew near. When the people entered the room I scanned their faces and could see that they were here for me. The last two people to enter the room were the men who had been here before.

Marlee broke the silence. "Talia, this is your Aunt Ruth and Uncle Shane and these two are the local police officers that located your family, Cedric and Benoit."

I hadn't known that I had an aunt and uncle and felt silly that I had not realised that the two men were the police. I wanted to run. I wanted the ground to open and swallow me. I looked around the room for another exit, as they were blocking the only clear way. Marlee sat beside me and placed her hand on my jiggling leg.

The woman stepped forward. "Hello, Talia. I'm your Aunt Ruth. Your mother was my sister."

She hesitated as I glanced at her.

Was? I blurted out, "I want my mummy and daddy."

The police officer Cedric stepped in. His face was serious as he knelt before me. "I am sorry, child. They are gone."

I looked into his yellow-stained eyes and said nothing, although I felt I was being torn apart. Pain surged through my core as the reality of what I already knew was thrust upon me. In the background, Ruth burst into tears and nuzzled her head into Shane's big strong shoulder. He rocked her from side to side while stroking her hair and gently kissing her forehead.

Marlee placed her hand on mine. "Look at me, child."

I turned my head to greet her eyes.

She too had tears streaming down her face.

"You will always be safe. You will always be protected. You will always be loved. Talia, you have to go with them now. They are your family. They will raise you."

"Why can't I stay here with you? I want to stay with you," I screeched. "Please don't send me away. I don't want to go."

Marlee reached out and drew me close to her bosom while heaving big choking sobs. "They are your family, Talia. You must go with them." She rocked me gently as we both cried.

Time seemed to be suspended. The anguish of the moment solidified the loss of my parents. I gulped for air through my sobs.

All my belongings had already been packed and were in the car.

Marlee held me close. "I have put some special things that you will need in a brown bag. Remember, child, you will forever be in my thoughts."

As we left, I stared at Marlee standing there on the porch waving to me until she was no longer visible. I had no idea where I was going, but I knew I would never forget where I had been.

At the airport Ruth and Shane checked in the bags while I watched a lady with a small brown dog walking up and down the queue, wagging its tail and sniffing everyone. It seemed like forever before we were seated on the plane. I had not said a word since we left. I nodded 'yes' or 'no' and shrugged my shoulders for anything I didn't know. That was to be the extent of my vocabulary for the entire journey. While they slept, I lay awake staring out the window. I wanted to get lost in the darkness.

***

After in excess of twenty-two hours on the plane, we finally landed. The bags were picked up and we were on our way. The journey in the car felt like another lifetime. I had not slept and my eyes felt like sandpaper. I wanted to curl up in a safe place and sleep forever. I hung my head out the window to feel the breeze against my skin. It wasn't long before the suburban houses were replaced by open expanses of land filled with animals I had not seen before. I was grateful for the visual curiosities that distracted me.

"Wake up, Talia. We're here," said Ruth.

I slowly opened my eyes and peeled my face from the side of the car door. The seat belt had left an indentation in my skin. Ruth opened my car door, stretching her arm out to offer me her hand. In a daze, I undid my seat belt and recoiled from her offer. I wasn't ready to come out yet. I folded my arms and sat still, looking at my feet.

I heard a noise and quick as lightning a little dog came from underneath the door, leaping into my lap.

Ruth laughed, "That's Scamper, our naughty Jack Russell."

He was a ball of energy on a mission to lick my face and stick his tongue in my mouth. I couldn't help but laugh as I tried to push him away. Scamper's tail wagged a million miles an hour and his joy was infectious. As quickly as he entered the car he exited. Leaping out of the car, he paused for a moment, turned to look at me and barked before he ran into the house.

Ruth left me in the car, suggesting that I come inside when I felt ready. I had no intention of ever leaving the car. After several hours it was my body that betrayed me; I needed to use the toilet. If I ignored the urge any longer I would piss my pants. It was time to alight from the vehicle. There was an initial rush of pain when the blood released to my legs. Then the pins and needles set in for a song and dance around my limbs before I could walk towards the doorway.

The entrance was long and narrow. I could hear the noise from a TV and voices coming from one of the rooms. I walked down the hall, looking from left to right in each open doorway, hoping to find the toilet.

Shane heard my footsteps and poked his head round the side of an archway. "You must be starved," he said with a gentle smile.

"I need to go to the toilet."

"Oh, of course you do. Here, follow me." With a sense of urgency he walked past another two doors and then extended his arm to the right, saying, "There you go. We'll be in the lounge room when you're finished, Talia. Ruth and I would like to introduce you to the rest of the family."

I scurried past him and just managed to pull my pants down and sit on the seat before what seemed like an endless stream of pee rushed out. It was a welcome relief to be free of the pressure built up in my bladder.

The hallway was clear. I wanted to make a beeline for the front door but Scamper came and started barking and dancing around my ankles.

I recognised Shane's voice. "Talia, we're in here."

I walked towards the sound of the TV and stood in the doorway of the room. Two boys sat on a couch and a girl sat on a beanbag.

They all looked at me and in a motley fashion said: "Hi", "Hello" and "G'day".

"Talia, I'd like you to meet our children: Thomas, Brad and Samantha. Tom is fourteen, Brad is ten and Sam is eight. Kids, this is Talia. She's six."

Tommy shuffled across the couch. "Talia, would you like to sit here?" He gestured to the space he had created beside him.

I placed a half-smile on my face and shook my head. I was tired and the last thing I wanted was the company of strangers.

"Come, Talia, you must be starving. Let me make you a sandwich and after that I'll show you around."

"No, thanks," I said in a barely audible voice. I stood there, looking at the floor, one hand wrapped around my midriff, the other clasping my shoulder. I was beyond exhaustion, feeling lost and alone. I had no idea where I was or who these people were. I wanted to sleep, where my dreams made sense to me.

"Talia, you have to eat something. It must be close to thirty-six hours since you had anything. Please, let me make you a sandwich." Shane dropped down on one knee so that he could have eye contact with me.

I shifted my gaze to a carpet stain.

"Okay, how about we compromise? If you drink a glass of milk, I will at least know that you have had something for your tummy to digest, hmm?"

"No, please." I turned to head into the hallway and out the front door.

I expected that Shane might stop me but he didn't. Perhaps he knew that I just needed some space. I sat on the edge of the porch and looked into their back yard. Scamper came out and sat beside me and placed his head on my lap.

"Scamper will stay like that all day and all night if you let him." I turned to see that Brad was now on the porch.

He sat on the other side of Scamper and patted him.

"We have five thousand hectares of land. Do you know how big that is?"

"No." I shook my head.

"It's pretty big. You could walk for ten days and ten nights and still not get from one end to the other." Brad paused. "Did you know it snows here?"

"No."

"Well, it does. Do you wanna see something?"

I continued to pat Scamper and shrugged my shoulders.

Brad jumped off the edge of the porch, reached out

for my hand and said, "Come on, Talia, I wanna show you something."

In a momentary flashback I could see myself standing in the classroom at the Union School on my first day when I met Bodhi. His hand extended, grabbing mine, leading me to my chair. I had not thought of Bodhi in almost forever. So much had happened since he had left.

"Come on, Talia." Brad flicked his fringe away from his eyes.

I reached out and grabbed his hand.

"Finally!" he exclaimed in a huff and proceeded towards a narrow track leading into the bushland.

After a few minutes we arrived at a small creek bed with beautiful crystal clean water gambling through it. I reached down and ran my fingers in the water. It was cold to the touch.

"That's pure mountain water. It doesn't get better than this." He stood with his hands on his hips and his face beamed with pride. He walked across to the other side of the shallow part of the riverbed, looking down into the water.

He gestured with his hand and whispered, "Talia, come over to me quietly. Try not to splash or you'll scare him."

I walked across to Brad and stood behind him, looking into the water where his gaze held steadfast and saw the most amazing little creature. It was adorable and so busy foraging that it didn't seem to notice or care that we were standing above it.

"This is Barry, the Platypus. I found him, so I named him."

"Hello, Barry," I said as I waved at the little creature.

Brad grabbed my hand to stop the waving. "You might scare him. He may be a little fella, but he has poison that he can use to get ya. Keep still, okay?"

I nodded and stayed frozen in position. I looked in amazement at this wondrous little creature while Brad told me everything there was to know about platypuses. I could have listened to him babble on for hours. He provided me a welcome distraction and he had no expectation or desire for me to contribute to the conversation. It was just what I needed.

As we walked back towards the house I realised that I was smiling and did not feel as sad.

Ruth was on the porch. Brad ran up to her and gave her a cuddle and told her that he had just taken me to meet Barry.

"Did you like Barry, Talia?"

I smiled. "Yes, he's lovely."

I could see that Ruth was relieved that I had responded and was smiling. She picked up Brad, gave him a big kiss and a cuddle and said, "Well done."

She gestured for me to come inside so I walked past her and into the hallway.

"Your bedroom is ready. I've placed all your things in there. You must be exhausted."

I had forgotten how tired I was. When I walked into the room that was to be mine I felt overwhelmed with exhaustion.

"I know you said you're not hungry, but Shane has made you that sandwich. You do need to eat. Please try. You know where the toilet is. I've left you a towel at the end of your bed in case you want to take a shower. Everyone has a designated toothbrush. Yours is the orange one in the stand on the sink. Okay?"

I looked across with sleepy eyes and said, "Okay. Thank you."

"If you need anything, we're down the hall. Sleep tight. We'll see you in the morning."

With that she closed the door behind her and left me standing in the room. I flicked off my shoes and socks and flopped onto the bed. I am not sure that I was even awake long enough for my head to hit the pillow. It was time to sleep.

Formative Years

It didn't take long for Brad and me to become thick as thieves. He had a way of knowing how to get me to do the things that Shane and Ruth wanted. A classic example was my refusal to eat with any regularity. Days could pass with me only partially eating an apple. I didn't know back then that my association to food and grieving were linked. I felt the depth of my loss in the presence of emptiness, which was amplified when I allowed myself to be starved. The moment that I ate something I felt better. I never wanted my parents' absence to be forgotten, so I would cycle through phases of feast and famine.

Brad's solution was to take me out on adventures. He taught me how to safely retrieve fresh honey from wild bees. He created damper and put it in the fire pit that Shane had built for us. The smell of fresh dough piping hot with liquid gold honey oozing from the bread was impossible to resist. We picked bush fruit from around the property and had picnics, pretending that we were eating to survive in the wild. Our adventures were an endless source of wonder and entertainment.

Tommy and Sam sometimes joined us on our quests. They too enjoyed the adventures that Brad would lead us on. An epiphany struck me when we were all at the edge of the creek bed sitting on some rocks with our toes dangling in the icy cold running water. Brad was in the middle of telling another of his fantastic stories. It felt great to be there amongst them. They wanted me there and I felt that I wanted to be there. It was nice.

On Sam's fourteenth birthday she was given a horse called Papa JoJo. It was a white Arabian cross that had a flowing mane and tail. I had never been in the presence of a horse before and was captivated by its majesty. Shane had built some yards close to the house for Papa JoJo to stay. I spent every waking moment I could with him and Sam was kind enough to let me. In fact, she probably thought she was taking advantage when I would volunteer to do all her Papa JoJo chores, such as mucking the yards, grooming him, washing out his water trough. The truth was that I wanted to be near him. I needed to be near him.

My obsession didn't go unnoticed by Shane and Ruth. They saw that I was completely committed to Papa JoJo's care and as a result they kindly bought me a little grey mare called Margret. She had been a schooling pony and had taught kids how to ride. The owner of the school was preparing to retire, so Shane took the opportunity to make an offer on Margret. I was twelve years old and for the first time in my life – truly happy.

Tommy was at university studying to become an architect. He would come home on some weekends to see the family, be spoilt with a hot meal and have all his laundry fluffed and folded. Brad was in his final year of high school. He was popular, received above-average grades and spent all his spare time on discovering girls. They swarmed to him like bees to honey. He had become quite the charmer. Sam too was entering a similar phase where she thought that boys, fashion and parties were a worthy pursuit. We may have been residing in the same household, but we were all now living distinctly separate lives.

Every morning before school I spent time with Margret and Papa JoJo. I rode them every chance I could and dedicated myself to acquiring all the knowledge that was available to obtain about horses. I drew pictures of them at school; I dreamt about them; I talked about them. They were everything to me. In their presence I felt grounded and at home.

From the age of fourteen through to my early twenties I worked every weekend and holidays at the local trail-riding school. I would ride Margret to work, round up the horses, brush them and get their tack on in preparation for the day. People travelled from across the globe to this riding school in the Victorian High Country. It was here that I started to get reacquainted with foreign cultures. I believed that I had the best job in the world. I was in my element. On the odd occasion Brad would swing past to spend the afternoon with me, I would double-dink him on a school horse called Thunder. We roamed around the bush tracks for hours while I listened to him tell stories about his latest conquests. We were still thick as thieves when we were together.

For my twenty-first birthday, Shane and Ruth created a scrapbook of my life. When I unwrapped the gift, I was lost for words. I sat in silence looking at each of the carefully crafted pages that contained moments in time. Ruth had managed to find photos of her and my mum from their childhood. She had contacted my dad's parents in Europe and they had sent out images of him. She also had a few images from their wedding that she had retrieved from family and friends around the world. I looked at the pages that contained my mum and dad's birth certificates. I had never known my mum was born in Australia and that my dad was born in Japan.

"Japanese?" I said, looking at them both.

Aunt Ruth laughed. "He was born in Japan but his parents are of Hungarian and Polish descent. Your dad was born in Japan because they were stationed there for two years."

The information in the book indicated that my parents had found each other while Mum was travelling across Europe. She met Dad and they instantly fell in love, marrying shortly after. My birth certificate and baby passport were also in there. I was born in London, England. It was surreal to have all this information in one place. I felt a sensory overload at the importance of the discoveries contained within. The second-last page in the book was a list of names, email addresses and phone numbers. Inscribed at the bottom of the page was a message:

Each one of these people knew and has been touched by your mum and dad. When you are ready, you can reach out to them to get to know who your parents were from their eyes. There are many untold wonderful stories that need to be heard if and when you are ready to collect them.

On the final page was an envelope. Inside it was a pile of letters.

As I pulled them out, Ruth said, "These are the letters

that my sister wrote to me while she was travelling. Some of them were written before you were born, some when she met your father, others while she was pregnant with you and the remainder were written after you were born."

I looked at her through a kaleidoscope of tears and mouthed the words "thank you" as I put the letter on my chest and closed my eyes. This was more than I could ever have hoped for.

After dinner I went outside to sit on the porch. Just as I was about to get comfortable Brad came out and jumped off the landing in front of me.

He held out his hand with the cheekiest of grins. "Come, Talia, I want to show you something."

I laughed, grabbed his hand and followed him down our well-worn narrow tracks of fifteen years of adventure. We crossed the creek in our shoes and climbed the rocks on the other side to reach the meadow. We lay in the grass and stared up at the stars that were starting to reveal themselves now that dusk had settled across the horizon.

"So, how does it feel to be twenty-one?"

"Okay, I guess. No different really."

"What's next? You can't work at that riding school forever. Do you plan on going to uni at all?"

"Hmm, I don't think so."

"You should go to uni; it's one party after another."

"I don't want to party."

"What do you want?"

"I'm not sure. What's with all the pressure?" I said with a laugh.

"Do you have a boyfriend?"

"You know I don't."

"I'm surprised that no-one has swept you off your feet yet."

"I spend every spare moment I have working at the riding school and with my own horses. Besides, I'm not interested in anyone."

"I know a stack of guys that would give their left nut to go out with you. I've seen those blokes look at you at the riding school. They fall over themselves to help you."

I laughed. "So?"

"Why don't you go out with one of them?"

"Why do you care who I date all of a sudden?"

"I'm just curious. I tell you all about my conquests, but you never tell me about yours."

"There's not much to tell. I went out with a couple of guys during high school. They seemed to be into me; I wasn't as into them, so I was always breaking up with guys. I didn't like how it made them feel so I stopped dating."

"Okay, tell me one of your most embarrassing moments with a guy."

"Well, there was this one time. David Addles tried to kiss me when I was sixteen. We were walking across the football oval when he felt inspired to make a move."

"What happened?"

"He caught me by surprise and I punched him in the nose. He had two black eyes for weeks after that. I think that was the start and end of my high school love pursuits. All the boys were too scared to make a move after that."

We both roared with laughter and I was grateful that it was now dark, as I was going a deep shade of crimson while reciting this ridiculous event. It was time to turn the tables.

"How old were you when you kissed your first girl?"

"I started kissing girls when I was fourteen. I knew

what I was doing by the time I was sixteen and now, quite frankly, I'm an expert in the field," he said smugly.

Sarcastically I responded, "I'm sure you're a regular Casanova." I made a few kissing noises for the full effect.

Brad reached over and tickled me. I retaliated and we both wriggled to escape one another's onslaught.

Then it happened.

Panting and lying by my side, he looked at me.

His expression changed from laughter to seriousness. Our eyes met, his hand shifted the hair from the side of my face and he ran his finger across my right cheekbone down to the side of my jaw-line, cupping it gently with his masculine hand. Ever so softly, Brad ran his thumb across the outline of my top and bottom lip and made them separate as I exhaled.

"Brad."

"Shhh." He tilted his head and used his soft lips to grab my upper lip. In a gentle but swift motion he did the same with my bottom lip and then he kissed me. In a rhythmic motion our lips, tongues and mouths danced a slow breathtaking dance. The intensity of the pressure grew as he transferred his passion. I was unable to resist his touch and didn't want him to stop. I surprised myself as I became lost in the moment and made little groaning noises to indicate the stimulus of pleasure.

"Brad, Talia, are you out there?" came a voice from the darkness.

We both jumped up and looked at each other.

"Shit, fuck, balls," I said in a panic.

"Yep, we're here," Brad called out with total composure.

"What are you two nutters doing? Mum was getting worried and made me come and look for you."

"Sorry, Tommy, we were just shooting the breeze and I wanted to stare at the stars. Guess I lost track of the time. We'll come back now."

As I straightened myself out and went to walk forward, Brad wrapped his arm around my waist from behind and leant in against my body, gently kissing my neck. My legs became like jelly and I once again surrendered to his touch.

He whispered, "I told you I was good."

"I can't see you guys. Are you coming yet?" Tommy called impatiently.

"YESsss," hissed Brad as he released me.

Tommy's torch lit the track ahead; I was behind Tommy with Brad beside me. In the black of the night he held my hand and had his head resting on my shoulder as we walked. It was unlike other times we had held hands.

This time it was arousing.

***

The next day I did my level best to ensure that I didn't act any differently around Brad. I wanted us to create a space where we could move forward from our indiscretion. I assumed that he too had concluded the same because he did not seem to give any sign that things were different. I remember feeling a little disappointment mixed with a dash of relief.

In the afternoon they all decided to do a family trip to the movies. I chose to stay home because it was rare to have the place to myself and lately I had been yearning for some peace and quiet. They all piled into the car and headed down the road. I went into the kitchen and set the kettle to boil.

"You didn't actually think I was going to leave you here alone, did you?"

Startled, I turned to see Brad standing in the doorway looking very sexy in his faded denim jeans, tight white singlet top and unbuttoned checkered shirt. I could feel myself flush. I didn't want him to notice that my heart had just skipped a beat and my stomach had butterflies.

"Hey, you, I'm making a cup of tea. Would you like one?"

Without a sound, he glided effortlessly across the room to be by my side. He ignored the question, leaning in to kiss my neck. I could feel his breath on and in my ear. I wanted to have the strength to make him stop his efforts to swoon me and yet I made no attempt to resist. I tilted my head so my lips could greet his. Interlocked in a passionate kiss that made what we were doing the evening before pale in comparison, Brad shifted his body to stand before mine. He pressed his hard muscular physique against me, running his expert hands from the base of my neck down my spine to the cleft of my buttocks. I tingled all over from his touch.

I once again released uncontrollable groans of pleasure that seemed to send him into an attentive frenzy. There was no warning as he lifted me onto the kitchen bench. One hand remained grasped firmly around my lower back while his other explored the base of my abdomen and headed up to caress the outline of my breasts. In a single move he pulled my singlet top down to reveal my left breast. He dropped his head and took my bosom in his mouth, using his tongue to play with my hardening nipple. He gently pulled my hair back so my body arched forward, allowing my breast to plunge deeper into his mouth. He released my other breast to attend to both of them like a seasoned pro.

In the background the kettle whistled madly.

Panting, I reached across and placed both hands on his head. I whispered, "We have to stop."

He too was breathless. "I know, I know."

I slid off the kitchen bench and walked across to the stove to turn it off. As I turned, Brad was bent forward on the bench with his head on his hands, still panting.

"Do you want a cup of tea?"

"No," he responded, shaking his head.

I abandoned the kettle. I no longer wanted a cup of tea either. I felt as though I had a family of circus creatures practising their new routine in my stomach and the excitement of the moment had my panties saturated with the juices of expectation. I was torn by lustful aches of desire that would have me proceed, yet there were the looming moral dilemmas of who we were.

Brad was still leaning over the bench. I walked across and placed my hands on his back and my head on my hands.

"We have to stop."

"I know," he said with a whimper.

"It's okay. We can pretend this never happened."

Brad shook his head from left to right as he slowly came upright. I reached across to turn him around. I needed him to look at me. When he did, I was shocked to see his bloodshot eyes filled with streams of tears. I started to well up too and buried my head into his chest, squeezing him tight.

"No, it's not okay." There was a pause and then he said, "I'm in love with you, Talia."

Nodding, I said, "I love you too."

"No, Talia, I am in love with you. I always have been. Ever since I was ten years old you have been everything to me. I tried to distract myself with all these other girls. Nothing seems to work. When I see you I'm right back where I started and now I'm so fucked up. I don't know what I'm going to do. I desperately want someone that I can't have. That I shouldn't have."

I didn't know what to say so I stated the obvious, "First cousins."

"Yep," was all he said in response.

We stood in one another's arms in silence for a while. Brad eventually sat down on the kitchen floor, leaning up against the cupboard. I sat between his legs with my back against his chest. He wrapped his arms around me and had his hands intertwined with mine. We talked for the remainder of the afternoon and well into the evening. It was raw, open, honest and beautiful. He had evoked such emotion in me. I could feel the depth of his desire as he recalled moments we had shared during our childhood. I had been totally oblivious to the extent of his love and admiration for me. I never knew it was possible for someone to find me amazing, mysterious and beautiful. I knew our window of time in one another's arms was drawing to a close. The rest of the family would be home any minute. I was overwhelmed with sadness knowing that nothing about this space we had created for one another was sustainable.

***

The next morning when I woke, Shane and Ruth were in the kitchen reading a letter that Brad had left them. It didn't say where he was going, just that he needed to go and explore the world for a while. He said he loved them, not to worry and that he would be in touch when he reached his first destination.

I wanted to die.

Discovery

Thanks to the scrapbook I now knew that I had living grandparents on my father's side: a Hungarian grandfather and a Polish grandmother living in Hungary. My mum's parents were deceased and their only children were my mum and Auntie Ruth, who had both been born and raised in Australia. Their family money had been made during the gold rush era, selling supplies to the miners. My dad was born in Japan. His father had a temporary posting there while his wife was pregnant. Their surname was Jacobs, which meant that was my surname too. Miss Talia Temperance Jacobs. All these years I had been using the surname Parker because Shane and Ruth thought it would be easier if they aligned my name to theirs. It was a way of protecting me from having to explain why my surname was different.

This just confirmed that I was completely clueless about my origins. I couldn't relate Talia Jacobs to me. I felt I was Talia Parker. Was that in essence a betrayal of my father's name? I was not sure how I felt about the middle name Temperance either. Seriously, what were my folks thinking? There was a swell of emotion welling in the pit of my stomach. I felt a surge of anger at their untimely death. If they hadn't have been so self-serving then perhaps they would still be alive. I would never have come to this place and Brad would not be roaming the world trying to forget me. With this, I buried my head in my pillow, burst into tears and sobbed myself to sleep.

***

"Talia, you're not eating again. What's wrong?" Shane was sitting on the edge of my bed. I had not heard him come in so I was a little startled to see that he was right there. "Is it Brad? I know you two are close."

I shrugged and then nodded. "He didn't even say goodbye."

"I know, sweetie. It's hard on all of us. Brad is his own man. He's a free spirit. That's what we all love about him. I have no doubt he'll get what he needs to out of his system and then he'll come home."

I tried to muster a smile for Shane. He had been so good to me all these years. He was always accepting, never trying to push me to align to their values. He just patiently watched over me when I became distant and trusted that I would find my way back to them. It was a special skill. I could see a lot of Brad's qualities in him.

"Ruth and I need to show you something. Can you meet us in the kitchen, please?"

I climbed out of bed and walked into the kitchen. I could see that Ruth had been crying, the telltale sign of moist eyelashes stuck together. There was an opaque dried glistening trail where the salty tears had paved their escape down the contours of her face.

Shane reached from under the table.

"Talia, we have something for you."

He brought an envelope to the surface and placed it on the table, sliding it towards me. I looked down at it and hesitated.

With an encouraging smile, Shane said, "It's a good surprise, Talia. Open it."

Inside the envelope there was a beautifully presented document on quality parchment paper. It had ornate scroll and gold etching around the border. At the top of the page, the title was bold and clear:

The last will and testament of Collette and Peter Jacobs.

I looked across at Shane, puzzled. *How could this be a good thing?* This piece of paper was a reminder that my parents were dead. Up until recently I hadn't even known their names: Collette and Peter.

"You're twenty-one, Talia. The trust that they set up for you is now accessible. You are their sole benefactor. The estate is yours."

It had never dawned on me in all those years that my parents would have anything to give. We had lived the life of nomads, wandering gypsies. Sure, we stayed in hotels and, from what I recalled, the houses they rented were nice, but I don't remember anything other than our travel cases as our possessions.

"Can I read this in my bedroom?"

"Of course," he said with enthusiasm.

Ruth reached out and touched my arm. "Talia, we didn't keep this from you. We just wanted to let you know when the time was right. Feel free to ask us any questions that you may have."

I replied, "Okay," to Ruth and headed for my room.

Sitting on the edge of my bed, I stared at the envelope. My heart sank as I positioned my body to slide down onto the floor with my back leant up against the bed. Closing my eyes, I imagined that I was leaning against Brad's chest. I wanted to feel his arms wrapped around me all warm and secure.

I whispered into the air, "I wish you were here."

Then I opened my eyes and took out the document. There was a load of legal jargon and terminology that I skipped over until I came to the section where it listed the assets. I wasn't sure what to make of what was written there. It seemed like I was reading something from someone else's life. How was this possible? I was astonished at the suggested wealth beyond my comprehension.

- Manor in Hungary on a 500-acre parcel of land
- Transylvania, Romania 300-acre parcel of land
- Apartment in central London
- Investments: paintings, sculptures, jewellery, stocks and bonds

Was this real? How was this possible? I felt as though I had landed in one of those email scams where I was bequeathed millions of dollars by Abdar Jamal Sameer of Tanzania. If I supplied my details, they would transfer the monies to me.

I stared at the words: *to Talia Temperance Jacobs we do bequeath solely our entire estate.* This just cemented the fact that I didn't know my parents at all and what little I remembered of them wasn't a true representation of who they were. I know that I should have been excited. According to this, I was set for life. I was set for ten lives, yet none of this mattered. All I could feel was the absence of two people I hardly knew but loved implicitly and now Brad was gone too. Was my destiny to be enveloped in riches in the absence of love?

***

During the following weeks, Shane went with me to set up bank accounts, apply for a passport and to work out how to best proceed with the management of my newly acquired estate. It had still not sunk in that I was now independently wealthy.

There wasn't a day that went by that I didn't think about Brad. It had been a couple of months since he'd left and we still hadn't received word of where he was. As I walked the well-worn paths I reminisced about all the moments we had shared: laughter, stories, our amazing bond. I knew Brad leaving was the best solution for both of us. I understood this because I ached for him to return. I had no desire to distance myself from him and would melt in his arms if he let me have my time over. It was in his absence that I realised that I too was in love with him.

Margret and Papa JoJo provided me a sense of grounding. I loved that they were always there for me. In the morning when I went out to feed them they would be waiting at the gate in anticipation. They had learnt my tricks and were now experts in the game of 'find the carrot'. It didn't matter where I hid it on my person they would home straight in for the reward. Simplistic joy.

One afternoon I was sitting on the edge of my bed and I noticed my old suitcase tucked up high on top of my wardrobe. I climbed up on the chair and retrieved the old fellow. I remember as a child insisting on carrying it myself, using two hands to drag it from place to place. It was almost as big as I was then and very heavy. Fifteen years on, I appraised it with new eyes and realised how tiny it was. Perspective is a marvellous thing.

The only contents were a brown paper bag and a clump of melted wax. I picked up the wax and held it in my left hand. My body heat transformed the cold surface to a soft warm texture. Images of a room came flooding back to me. The words 'truth, honesty, protect, serve' were audible in a whisper. The name 'Marlee' chanted in my mind's eye. I couldn't recall what she looked like, but I could feel the warmth of her presence now. Haiti had been a lifetime ago.

I opened the crumpled brown bag. There was a beautiful symbol drawn in white on a piece of yellowed paper, a dry blood-stained white feather, a rock, a candle and a plaited piece of hair intertwined with a turquoise and orange ribbon. I knew that there was symbolism associated with all that was before me, but I struggled to understand what it was supposed to represent. Why would the old lady pack these things and send me away with them?

I placed the suitcase under my bed and left my room to see what Ruth and Shane were up to. They had received a postcard from Brad. He had been travelling around Europe and posted it from Madrid. It didn't say much, other than he was seeing loads of amazing sites, meeting some interesting people and loving the change of scenery. The renewed energy that Brad's letter had brought to them was obvious in their demeanour. It was a relief to know that he was well and from the little he had written it appeared that he was having a fantastic journey. I was glad that he was all right. I missed him desperately.

"Talia, there's a letter here for you too. It looks like it's from Brad."

I could see that Ruth was hoping I would open it in front of her. I understood her hunger for more knowledge about her son. I just knew that I couldn't provide her with that comfort until I had read the contents myself to see if it was clear to share. I reached out and took the letter and walked out the front door. My body felt as though it was going everywhere all at once and it was only my skin that was keeping me from falling apart. My instinct told me that this letter was a belated goodbye. As I walked down towards the creek, tears streamed down my face. I yearned to hear his voice and kiss his lips. I sat on our rock, put my feet in the water, took a deep breath and opened the envelope. It was a single page with an insignia at the top:

With Compliments Stamford Hotel.

Dear Talia,
I left abruptly without saying goodbye. I knew that if by chance you asked me to stay that I wouldn't have the willpower to leave. Mere words could not possibly describe the infinite sea of roses that passes between your ruby lips. You are my perfection.

I don't know how to change how I feel about you. I know that I shouldn't act upon my desire to be with you. This leaves me feeling like I need to fight to breathe. That's why I left without saying goodbye. It's also why I've decided that I won't return until I've fallen in love with another. I'm not sure if that's even possible. Talia, I have to try.

I hope that someday you will find it in your heart to forgive me. In return, I hope one day I can find it in my heart to forgive myself. I feel as though I betrayed your trust and took advantage to satisfy my own insatiable desire to be with you. I wish I had been stronger than that for you.

Just know that wherever you are and whatever you choose to do that you are always loved by me.
Brad

I read the words over and over. I felt as though my heart had been ripped out of my chest. I couldn't determine whether I was better or worse off now that I had his intentions confirmed. I folded the paper and placed it under a rock beside the riverbed. Walking into the water, I lay face down with my eyes held tight and my breath trapped deep in my lungs. I didn't surface until my body forced me to seek new breath. I sat in the shallows of the river and let the water rush past me. I needed to feel something other than the pain of the words that swilled around my brain.

"Talia, Talia, you need to come quick!" Ruth called in the distance. She sounded distressed.

I jumped up and ran towards her voice. Partway down the path, we met.

Her chest was heaving to catch her breath. "It's Margret, she's …"

I didn't wait to hear the rest. I bolted towards the stables. There was my baby girl rolling on the ground and making awful noises.

Shane looked at me and said, "It's colic."

"I know what it is," I snapped as I walked towards her.

Kneeling down, I placed my head on her stomach. There was no noise. This wasn't a good sign. I could tell that she was in a lot of pain.

"The vet is on his way," Shane said as he stepped back.

"Okay, thanks, Shane. Sorry – I didn't mean to snap."

He just smiled and told me to let him know if I needed help.

I managed to get Margret on her feet and walked her around. A van came screeching down the driveway, leaving a cloud of dust in its wake. It was the vet; he had finally arrived.

"Hi, Talia, how is she doing?"

"She's been walking for the last thirty minutes, but her breathing is laboured and I can't hear any noises in her gut."

"Okay, let me have a listen."

The vet examined her and suggested that we try to flush out her stomach to get things unblocked and moving again. I held her while the tube was fed through her nose and into her stomach. He poured the liquid solution down the tube and waited. After ten minutes he checked her vital signs and confirmed that she wasn't responding. He reassured me that it wasn't uncommon for a horse not to respond to the first treatment. As he tried to administer the next dose she reefed back and lay down on the ground, rolling back and forth. Her legs were flailing and she was clearly in an enormous amount of pain.

"Talia, it's clear to me that she's twisted her bowel. I could offer you surgery, but at her age and with the amount of pain she's in I think the kindest thing to do would be to put her down."

"Give her something to ease her discomfort and try again," I said in desperation.

"No. Honestly, Talia, it's time."

With that, Margret let out an enormous blood-curdling groan.

I looked at the vet and nodded my head, resigned to the fact that she was telling me that she needed to be released from the pain.

"You're doing the right thing." He walked over to his car and prepared the needle.

I knelt beside her, holding her head in my lap. I stroked her face and kept saying the words, "Thank you for everything. I love you, I love you so much, I love you."

"Talia, you need to leave now. This is unfortunately not a pretty process. It's best if you go inside and I'll handle it from here."

"Just do what you need to do. I'll stand over here out of your way. Don't block her view of me. I need her to know that I'm here. She needs to be able to see me."

He looked at me, shook his head and then knelt down to find the vein in her neck. He administered a lethal dose of a barbiturate that would instantly stop her heart and breathing muscles. Once all the dark green contents were in, he jumped back. Margret was still lying down on her side. For the longest moment nothing happened and then she made a god-awful noise, reefing for air. Her legs frantically moved, as if in an attempt to gallop away. It took minutes before she passed and longer for the involuntary muscle twitching to stop. The vet checked her once more and nodded his head to confirm she had passed. Her transition from life to death was so undignified. There was nothing humane about it.

The vet did an obligatory pause and then muttered, "I'm sorry for your loss," and walked out of the yard.

I had no strength to acknowledge his words. I was numb with my own pain, guilt and shame. I knelt back down next to her, closed her eyes and put her tongue back in her mouth. I placed one hand on her chest and one on her head and closed my eyes. Margret lay there perfectly still. I felt empty inside; I had nothing more in my life to lose. In that moment it seemed crystal clear to me that nothing that I loved was able to last.

In the background I could hear the vet driving off and the tractor engine starting. I knew that it was Shane setting off to find a spot where he could use his backhoe to dig a big enough pit to drop the old girl in. As I walked across the yard, he looked at me. He mouthed the word "sorry" and then focused on the task at hand. I nodded and walked inside.

Ruth was in the lounge room. I could hear her sobbing.

I stood at the doorway and said, "She's gone."

I could not bear to watch her cry and had no ability to console her when I was unable to console myself. I was still drenched from my cleansing in the river. I peeled out of my clothes and hopped into a piping hot shower. Resting my head against the cold tiles, I let my body be enveloped by the steam and water. My head hurt. I could not possibly shed another tear or feel another emotion.

***

Deep in my sleep that evening I was surrounded by the

rhythmic beat of drums. I could not see where they were coming from or who was creating the sound. The beat grew louder and louder and I felt drawn to the resonance. I struggled to locate the source. The more I tried to reveal where it was coming from the further they were from me. When I relaxed and enjoyed the sound it came closer and grew louder.

***

In the morning I leaped out of bed, inspired; I knew what I needed to do. I took some matches from the kitchen and all the items that were in my crumpled brown paper bag. I walked barefoot through the bush to the river, letting the earth squeeze between my toes. The dappled sunlight danced on my face and I welcomed the crisp morning air into my lungs.

At the edge of the river I lifted the rock where I had left Brad's letter. I placed the candle on the flat river rock that we both used to sit on. Pulling out the piece of yellowed paper with the symbol drawn in white, I placed the blood-stained white feather diagonally across the symbol, with the rock on top of it. I lit the candle and placed it near the items.

Kneeling beside my collection of things, I unfolded the letter and placed it against my heart. I closed my eyes and inhaled the clean eucalyptus-infused aroma in the air.

When I exhaled I said the words, "I release you."

I placed it over the flame.

As it caught on fire I smiled and then spoke the words out loud so that the breeze could carry my message: "Fall in love with another; be happy."

As the paper transformed, I let the ash float away

with the current and watched the smoke rise and dissipate. As the ashes from his letter drifted further away the sound of the drums in my mind's eye grew louder. It was time.

***

When I arrived back at the house, I placed a few of my things into a small pack and left it beside the front door. I walked into the sunroom where Shane and Ruth were having their breakfast. Giving them a cuddle, I said that it was time for me to go. They didn't seem surprised.

I honestly had no idea where I was heading.

I only knew for certain that I had to go.

Freedom

Driving down the road heading towards the city, I could feel the excitement of the unknown. I had the roof down on my old bright-yellow converted Volkswagen Bug, the radio blaring and I was singing at the top of my voice. I made up the words if I didn't know them; no rules. This was my time to decide on my future. The sun shone on a perfect blue-sky day. In this moment I was invincible.

It took a few hours to reach the heart of Melbourne. I parked my car in a narrow undercover concrete structure that felt like a dungeon. When I eventually managed to find my way out of the labyrinth I headed out to explore the big smoke. My first stop was the Queen Victoria Market. My senses were alive with the colour, textures and noise. It was nothing like the farmers' markets in rural Victoria. I found myself drawn to a section of the market that sold small goods. I had never seen so much food in one place.

It took me hours to look at every stall. My feet ached and my belly was starting to rebel against the variety of rich foods that I now had swilling in my stomach. I knew better but still insisted on ordering a Spanish doughnut to try. One bite of that oily sweet delight started the worst series of guttural cramps. I knew that it was time to leave and, more importantly, to find a place to stay for the night. Judging by how my body was reacting, I suspected that a toilet with a view would be sufficient for the evening.

Weaving through the streets admiring the architecture, I noticed the sign for the Stamford Hotel. My body had hot flushes and I could feel beads of sweat forming on my brow. At first I associated this to the fact that Brad had written to me on some stationary that had the same name. My body quickly synchronised with my mind, sending pain through my core, complete with loud guttural noises that said – find a toilet or shit yourself. I organised a room at the Stamford, spending the larger portion of the evening as promised on the toilet, expelling the demons that possessed my bowels. The unexpected delight was involuntarily throwing up into the bath tub in front of me. A kaleidoscope of infused colours oozed down the drain. Oh, that smell was simply not human. I was thankful when my system settled down and I could have a hot shower. I crawled into bed and drifted off to sleep.

***

During the passing weeks, I familiarised myself with the city centre and the surrounding inner-city suburbs. I was drawn to the amazing atmosphere of places like the cafés in Richmond, pubs in Brunswick Street, Fitzroy and restaurants in Fitzroy Street, St Kilda. This environment was the polar opposite of where I had lived. Openly gay people walked the streets holding hands; body art and piercings seemed to be the norm. I surprised myself when

I started to notice men in torn jeans and dreadlocks. It was all a welcome distraction from the recent events. Change was definitely a stimulus that I now understood I needed to retain in my life.

Eventually I moved out of the hotel and rented a room in Richmond just off Bridge Road. My two house mates, Denis and Rhonda, were third generation Aussies. They worked hard, partied even harder and would find any excuse to drink.

"Yippee! It's Monday. I'll drink to that."

Seriously, I am not exaggerating when I say that they were total piss-heads. Up until then, I had not had a drink, so I was completely unaware of what my alcohol tolerance would be.

The Night Cat became a regular haunt. We headed down late in the evening and stayed until closing. It was fashionable to party at the witching hour. Rhonda and Denis had it down to a fine rhythm. After work they would go to the gym for a workout. Then they would come home, have a sleep and then visit the Night Cat. The crowd varied depending on what was being hosted. One of my favourites of the week was 'Thursday salsa'. The place would be packed with people all dressed in tight clothes that showed off their form. They would move with hypnotic synchronicity. I was an avid admirer of the skill and timing that was required to execute this style of dance.

One evening I was sitting with the guys in our usual spot. It was in a great position that allowed us to witness the talent entering and exiting the venue. There was a clear view of the dance floor and, thankfully, it was far enough away from the toilets so we didn't get a waft of the combination of urine and the bleach they used to mask it seeping into the atmosphere.

I was sipping on my vodka and lime when I noticed a guy walk in the door. He had a girl on his arm and two more followed behind. The little hairs stood up on the back of my neck when he looked straight at me and smiled.

I wasn't expecting that.

A hot flush rushed through my core as I averted my eyes, hoping that he hadn't noticed my reaction to his gaze. When I turned my head again he was at the bar ordering a drink. The bartender giggled as she leaned in to flirt with him. He seemed to politely engage in conversation with her but didn't project a vibe that told me he was interested. When she passed him his drink he reached across to take a mouthful and turned to look at me again. I freaked out and spun round so that he had a view of my back. Denis was on the dance floor making his moves on a girl and Rhonda was at the table with me, annihilating her liver as she did with a frequency that fascinated me.

"Rhonda, there's this really hot guy that came in and …"

"Huh, where?" She looked around like a meerkat on the scout.

"Don't make it obvious," I said in a scolding tone.

"What does he look like? I'm not sure who I'm looking for?" she said, totally ignoring my request.

"He's really tall and is standing at the bar: dark hair, great smile."

Rhonda smiled as she said in a teasing voice, "He's not there anymore." She laughed loudly like a mad hatter.

I turned to see him standing behind me wearing the cheekiest smile.

"Hi, can I join you ladies?"

"Sure, sure. Come sit with me," slurred Rhonda as she slapped the leather on the seat beside her. "I'm Rhonda and this is Talia."

"Talia, what a beautiful name," he said as he sat down beside Rhonda.

"I'm Ethan. Do you come here often?" He looked straight at me, trying politely to ignore the way Rhonda was leaning into him and fondling the buttons on his shirt.

Rhonda answered, "We come here all the time. This is our Cat at night: the Night Cat. You could call us pussies of the night." She screeched with laughter.

I smiled and shook my head slightly. She was smashed.

"Talia, would you like to dance?"

I looked across at him and before I could respond his eyes gestured at Rhonda as he said, "Please?"

Laughing at his expression, I said, "Sure."

We walked towards the dance floor; I felt butterflies in my stomach. I was clueless about how to execute salsa moves and knew that this was not something that I was going to be able to wing. I had watched others in admiration but had never thought to try it myself. As I turned, he stepped into my space.

I stepped back and blurted, "I don't know how to do this. Can we go to the bar instead?"

"Just as well that I'm an instructor then." He once again stepped into my space and this time placed my hands in position.

***

That evening was the first of many we would spend together dancing. He was an amazing teacher and found a way to translate the moves so I could visualise them and eventually feel them. Salsa aroused a flirtatious sensuality that surprised me. The dance moves were so tactile that at times I would find myself blushing.

Ethan could sense these moments and would say in a sultry deep voice, "You need to surrender to the dance. In this space, the men lead and the women follow."

***

It was the week before Valentine's Day almost twelve months since I had first met Ethan.

Rhonda and I were in the lounge chatting about the usual when she asked, "Have you done it with Ethan yet?"

I looked at her and then shyly said, "No."

"Oh, my god, Talia, what are you waiting for? He's so friggin hot!"

"I don't know. I honestly don't know." I shrugged my shoulders.

"Okay, girl, you have to decide on a date and then we have to get you groomed for the occasion."

"Date? Groomed?"

"Yeeeesssss. Okay, next week is Valentine's Day. That can be your gift to him."

"What? Sex?"

"Not just sex, honey, your cherry … POP." She made a noise with her mouth and laughed.

I looked at her with an expression of distain. "What do you mean by grooming?" I needed to distract her from discussing my virginity any further.

"You know …. mani, pedi, wax, the whole kit and caboodle," she said with one hand on her hip and the other waving in a large circular motion up and down.

Without allowing me another word, she was off to make phone calls to book time at her favourite salon.

***

In my bedroom I lay on my bed in the darkness searching for answers to explain my hesitation. Ethan was sweet, loving, sexy and totally enamoured of me. What more did I want? Girls would melt in his presence, desperately trying to get his attention. He seemed to be blind to their attempts. When I walked into a room he would light up. It made me feel incredibly special. I could drink in the gaze offered from his green eyes. There were moments of frustration when we kissed passionately; he would lean into me and grind against me. I would also find myself getting worked up but something always stopped me. I wasn't ready to do anything with him or anyone else yet.

A week passed and I was at the salon and day spa with Rhonda. I had myriad people fussing over me: a hairdresser colouring my hair; a woman in front of me executing a pedicure; and two woman on the left and right of me giving me a manicure. Tinted eyelashes, tinted eyebrows: Rhonda was having a blast while I wanted this day to end. I had never been a tactile person. I didn't feel comfortable with all these strangers in my space pushing, pulling and prodding at me. Little did I know that the worst was yet to occur.

I was taken into the back room where a deceptively sweet-looking lady said that she would execute the facial mask for skin rejuvenation and the waxing for hair removal. I took off my jeans as she asked and lay on the table. She started with waxing my eyebrows, upper lip and underarms. I have never sworn so much in my life.

When the facial mask went on and the cucumber patches were placed on my eyes, I felt a welcome cool relief on my throbbing face. I could feel the beautician sprinkle talc on my legs and between my legs. I was a little surprised at how close her hand was rubbing to my nether regions.

She felt me tense. "Just relax. I am going to start at your bikini line and work my way down."

As she spread my legs apart and placed the strips of warm wax on my bikini line I could feel some of the hairs pulling with the drag of the wax.

In my mind I was chanting *no, no, no.* The first strip was mercilessly ripped off as I screamed, "Mother fucker!"

She laughed. "Sorry, Talia, this is the price that we women pay for beauty."

I was still in shock and was frantically trying to think of an excuse to make her stop.

"Oh, look – you have a little birthmark or mole here," she said, touching where she had just waxed.

"The only mole I know of is the one that booked me for this."

We both laughed and she continued her torturous method of removing the hair from my body. By the time it was finished, my new haircut and blowdry was plastered to my head from the sweat. I was exhausted and just wanted to sleep.

"Next stop, Talia, we are going lingerie shopping," Rhonda said in her singing tone.

"I'm exhausted. I just want to go home. This was a bad idea. I feel like a mass of pain."

"Oh, don't be so melodramatic. That will pass in a half-hour or so."

Rhonda seemed to know all the cool places to go. She took me into a fabulous shop that specialised in nothing but beautiful undergarments. At the counter she announced that she was looking for something extraordinary for me as it was going to be my first time. The ladies behind the counter squealed and rushed over to me. I was so embarrassed. I wanted the ground to swallow me whole. Eventually, after an amount of fussing, goos and gars, I managed to find an outstanding outfit for the evening. It was a delicate, black, lightly laced, see-through nighty. The matching panties were in a boy brief cut that fitted perfectly. I was ready.

***

Valentine's day arrived. I kept myself busy across the day to distract myself from the fact that tonight was the night that I would surrender myself to a man for the first time. I had moments where my mind would drift to images of Brad and me in the kitchen. I had not allowed myself to think of him in the longest time.

In the afternoon I found myself dialling Ruth and Shane's number. I wanted to hear their voices; I needed to know if Brad had returned.

"Hello."

"Hi, Ruth. It's me."

"Talia," she said with a squeal. "How are you? It's been so long. I wish you would call more."

"I'm good, thanks. How is everyone?"

"Shane is great. Tommy just got promoted at the architecture firm. Sammy is struggling a bit with her final year of nursing, but you know her. She always finds her feet."

"And Brad?" I said in hope.

"Brad finally called us a week ago. He said that he's working his way across Europe as a bartender and has been offered a job on a cruise ship that he's considering. He seems happy enough."

"Did he say when he was coming home?"

"Sadly, no. I think for the moment we've lost Brad to the travel bug. I'm just relieved that he's okay."

"Has he met anyone?" I cringed as I said the words. I felt compelled because I wanted to know the answer.

"There was a girl's voice laughing in the background when he called. I asked him who it was, but he didn't really offer any information. You know Brad. He tends to keep his cards close to his chest."

"I'm going to have to go. I just wanted to give you guys a quick call to wish you a happy Valentine's Day. I hope that you have a fun night."

"You too, Talia. Come and visit when you're ready, okay?"

"Sure. I will. I promise."

I hung up the phone and burst into tears. I'm not sure what I was expecting to achieve through that call, but conjuring up all the emotions that I had suppressed about Brad was certainly not a conscious objective. I wanted to stop this feeling in the pit of my stomach from taking over my core. It was clear that I was self-sabotaging. I just didn't know how to stop.

I climbed in my car and drove, the top down, wind gusting and the radio blaring. I took myself to St Kilda pier. It was a spot that had an intangible familiarity to me. I walked down the weathered bridge towards the café. I took my takeaway coffee and headed for the end of the pier where I could sit wedged amongst the rocks and stare out into the bay.

Hours passed and eventually I dozed off. It was dusk by the time I stirred. There was drool down the side of my face and a cold chill on my back. Little glowing red eyes watched me while others scattered about their business. A nest of water rats also known as rakali surrounded me. They were known in the area and were most active in the evenings. I found them fascinating, as they were often compared to the platypus. These two species were known as the most specialised amphibious Australian mammals. I watched the rats dive into the water, using their partially webbed hind feet and tails as rudders as they foraged for food.

It was getting dark.

I had to go.

When I arrived back at the house I could see there was a hive of activity inside. I walked in the door and was bombarded with a united scolding.

"Where have you been?"

I looked across at Rhonda, who was already three sheets to the wind.

"Who are all these people?"

"Just some friends I invited back to have a little drinky poos," she said with a wink and a smile.

"Ethan was here but he left about an hour ago. He was pissed at you."

"Oh, shit Ethan."

I grabbed my keys and headed out the door to go to Ethan's. When I arrived at his house, there was no answer. The lights weren't on, so I could only assume he wasn't home. I drove around for a while and ended up at the Night Cat. He was sitting at the usual place surrounded by women all craving his attention. He looked across at me as I entered the room.

I mouthed the words 'I'm sorry' as I walked towards him.

I could see that he was unhappy and the girls were all now staring at me as though to keep me off their territory.

"Hey," was all I could conjure up.

He paused for a moment while he looked into my eyes. "Where were you? I wanted to surprise you tonight." He stopped mid-sentence then said quietly, "I waited for hours."

I reached across, grabbed his hands and motioned him to stand. I shifted his face so that his eyes were looking directly into mine.

"Ethan, I'm sorry."

The girls behind us snickered. I could feel their vulturistic minds wishing for him to tell me where to go. They wanted to see us argue so they could feast on opportunity. I put my arms around his neck and held him in my arms. He released a big sigh and ran his hands across my waist, pressing into the small of my back to draw me closer. We held each other for what seemed like an eternity.

I whispered into his ear, "Let's get out of here."

He released his grip and we headed out the door. We didn't speak. He jumped in my car, placed his seatbelt on and looked straight ahead. I paused for a moment and then started the car. As we headed down the road, I searched for options. I knew I couldn't bear to go home to what would no doubt be an unruly house party. Instead I found myself back at the pier.

This was the place in the city where I felt the most comfortable. I fetched a picnic blanket from the boot and led Ethan to the sandy banks underneath the pier. As I laid out the blanket, Ethan walked to the water's edge and stared out into the shimmering blackness. He had his arms folded.

I went to join him and wrapped my arms around his from behind, staring out into the water from across his shoulder. My thumb gently ran across the outline of his strong masculine hands. He eventually surrendered to my touch and I could feel the tension in his hand dissipate so I could intertwine my fingers with his.

I placed my head in the centre of his back between his shoulder blades as my hands found their way under his jacket and shirt to his bare skin. He didn't flinch at my cold touch. I travelled from his waist up to his back, towards his neck, and then used my nails to gently claw back down the path from which they had come. I motioned to lift off his shirt. Without resistance, he placed his arms in the air.

I let his clothes fall to the ground as I gently started to kiss his back. My hands felt as though they had a mind of their own as they danced across the outline of his shoulders then his arms and towards his chest. His chest expanded as he inhaled a deep breath when I lightly touched his small nipples. He turned to face me. In one swoop he had me cradled in his arms and was carrying me to the blanket. My heart pounded; goose bumps surfaced all over my body and followed an electric residue at the trail of his touch. I started to take deeper breaths. He was half on top of me with his chest pushed up against mine. I lifted my head to kiss his lips and he pulled away.

"Patience," he said as he stared deep into my eyes.

He ran his hand diagonally over my flat stomach then used his hand to trace the outside rim of my jeans. With a wicked grin on his face he dropped his body so his mouth could explore my belly button. The warmth of his lips gently kissing my body sent pulses of sensation all around. Using his tongue, he skipped across my abdomen, blowing his warm breath on me. It felt indescribably good.

As he lifted my top and released the clasp on my bra, I whimpered, "Kiss me."

Ethan positioned himself between my parted legs and lifted my upper body so my legs straddled his torso. His hand supported the back of my head as he pressed his lips hard against mine. I groaned loudly as his groin raised to grind against me. I was so wet and dizzy with the anticipation that I felt weak. I wanted to surrender to my desire.

Ever so gently Ethan placed me down in front of him. He maintained eye contact as he slowly unbuttoned my shirt. He opened my top to reveal my breasts loosely masked by my unclasped bra. He ran his right hand across the surface of my left breast. He then leant forward, lifted my bra so he could clasp my nipple between his pursed lips. I could feel his tongue tapping on it and as he lifted his head up he extended my breast into a taut mound. His other hand twisted, tweaked at my right nipple. I arched my body to grind against him. I ran my fingers through his hair and pushed his head into my breast.

I reached down and unbuttoned his jeans and grabbed his erect penis. My instinct kicked in as I started to rub my hand up and down the shaft. He groaned as his head rested on my shoulder, his back arched up and his waist lifted to provide me with better access.

I closed my eyes and whispered, "I want you inside me."

Ethan let out an elongated groan and with his eyes closed found my mouth and passionately kissed me. His hands worked to clumsily undo my jeans. He only disconnected from my lips to remove the remainder of our clothing and then he was there again, kissing me deeply. He placed himself in position and gently eased his way into my swollen aching vagina. At first I had a flushed intensity of pain that subsided quickly after he started to thrust in and out. He was on his elbows looking down at my torso rising to greet his motions. I pulled my legs apart as far as I could and wrapped them around him. I could feel the drippings of my body's excitement trail to the cleft of my arse. I was so aroused.

***

I woke to the sound of seagulls and footsteps on the pier. Ethan and I lay wrapped in the blanket on the sand.

"Ethan."

"Hmm," he said with his eyes still closed.

"It's morning and we're naked on the beach. We need to get up."

Ethan's eyes slowly opened and he stretched out his arms and legs. He looked at me and smiled.

"Morning, you."

"Morning," I said, biting my lower lip thinking about the night before.

I sat up and reached for my jeans, only to have Ethan grab them and throw them out of my reach. He had this look in his eye as he positioned on all fours and lunged on top of me, holding my hands firmly above my head.

Joyfully squealing, I said, "Ethan, no!"

"Shhhh," he said as he dropped his head down to nuzzle my breasts.

"Seriously, no. There are people walking about. We'll get sprung!"

Lifting his head to reveal a delicious smile, he said, "So?"

"Ethan, please," I implored in my sweetest voice. "I have sand in the crack of my arse and god knows where else. I really need to take a shower."

He burst out laughing, rolled onto his back and gestured that I was free to dress.

Forever

Time melted when we were together. It would soon be two years since we had met and it only felt as though weeks had passed. I wouldn't have known if it wasn't for Rhonda executing the countdown. I had never really placed much emphasis on birthdays, anniversaries and the like. Let's face it, if the department stores hadn't done a countdown to Christmas I could have easily let that slip by too.

I believed for the most part Ethan and I were happy. I enjoyed spending time with him and appreciated the space we had created for one another for sexual exploration. I found Ethan to be an attentive lover with moments of surprise. Most of all, I knew that he loved me.

On the eve of our second anniversary, he and I were lying in his bed.

"Talia, do you know that tomorrow will be our two-year anniversary?"

"Yep, Rhonda reminded me yesterday."

He laughed. "Is there anything special that you'd like to do?"

"I'm happy to chill after work, if that suits."

"Really? I thought you might want to go out for dinner or something."

"We can, if you want. Honestly, I'm happy to just go with the flow."

We sat in silence for a while. I could hear his breathing become irregular, deep sighs released into the darkness. I turned onto my side and placed my head on his chest.

"Talk to me, Ethan. What's wrong?"

At first he didn't respond. He just stroked my hair and lay in the still of the night. I had almost drifted to sleep when he broke the silence.

"I don't know anything about you, Talia. Tomorrow we'll have been together for two years and I actually know nothing about you. Whenever I try to ask you questions you say you don't want to talk about it. I don't even know what job you do. It's not normal." He paused as though to give me an opportunity to respond.

I lay still and listened.

He took a deep breath and in a broken voice whispered into my hair, "It's as though I'm in love with a ghost."

I lifted my head from his chest. "I'm not sure what you want, Ethan."

"I want you. I want all of you. I would like to think that one day you might look at me the way I look at you. It's like you choose to hold back to keep me hungry for more. What are you afraid of?"

I sat up and shifted across to climb out of bed.

"What are you doing?" He reached out to touch my hand.

I moved out of reach of his grasp and fumbled around for my clothes.

As I put them on, he growled, "Great. Well done,

Talia. I try to tell you how I feel and express my frustration about how little I know about you. Instead of talking to me, you're choosing to leave? Really?"

I stood in the doorway of his bedroom and leaned up against the door jamb.

"Ethan, I told you in the beginning. I'll never speak of my past because I don't feel the need to share it. You said it didn't matter but now clearly it does. Nothing has changed for me. I don't feel the need to share where I have been and, more importantly, I don't want to."

I paused to hear him sobbing in the darkness. My stomach churned. I wanted to hold him in my arms to console him. Against my better judgement, I walked across and lay beside him. He wrapped himself around my body, buried his head into my chest and released his emotions.

Tears silently streamed from my eyes. I couldn't bear to know that I was causing my sweet Ethan such pain.

"Don't leave me, Talia," he said with sad desperation.

"Shhh, I'm here, Ethan. I'm here," I said, rocking him gently from side to side.

He finally fell asleep. I lay beside him awake for most of the night. As dawn broke I squinted at the streams of light sneaking past the blinds. My eyes were swollen from crying and I had a thumping headache. Quietly I left the room and sat in the kitchen. I used my hands to support my aching head while I searched for what I should do. I needed space to gather my thoughts; my mind was clouded with sadness. I hated how I made him feel. I knew in my heart of hearts there was only one thing I could do.

Hours later, Ethan woke to find a note on the pillow where I used to lie.

Dear Ethan,

I feel blessed to have met you and to be a part of your life. There were times I would foolishly allow myself to daydream that we could be together forever. Last night you showed me that my lack of desire to share my past means something to you. I want to remain true to how I feel and not compromise myself in an attempt to appease you or anyone else. I have nothing to hide but also feel no need to share. I don't want to fight about it and I cannot bear to watch you in pain.

Thank you for loving me. You deserve to love and be loved. Let me go, find your truest forever.
Forgive me,
Talia

By the time Ethan had arrived at my house to look for me I was on a plane heading overseas. I had left Rhonda a note saying that I going walkabout for a few weeks but gave no other details.

I actually had no idea where I was going.

Initially, when I jumped into the car I got onto the Hume Highway to head towards New South Wales. On the way I saw a sign for Tullamarine airport. I found myself indicating and deviating towards the sign. As I parked the car and walked in I realised that this was the second time I had been here, and yet there was nothing familiar about this open sterile place.

The customer service desk clerk directed me to the local Blue Cloud travel agency. I sat with the agent and worked out where I could go. The two immediate choices were New Zealand or Thailand. The rest of the destinations required visa applications. I flipped a coin. Heads landed – Thailand. The agent seemed amused at my behaviour. I didn't care about the destination. I just needed to leave.

The moment I was seated on the flight I rested my head against the wall of the plane and fell asleep. The next time my eyes opened we had landed. The lady who sat beside me kindly tapped on my shoulder to wake me. Instinctually I followed the mass of people exiting the same flight. I went through customs, where a man spent a serious amount of time looking at my passport and then at my face.

When I looked around to see if everyone was having the same experience, he barked at me in broken English, "Eyes forward look, please."

Eventually he stamped my passport, handed it back and I was off to the baggage carousel.

Thankfully for me the travel agent had recognised that I was clueless and totally unprepared for my spontaneous journey. He had arranged for a driver to pick me up from the airport and take me to the resort. It took forty-five minutes on a very bumpy road. There were no streetlights so I could only see glimpses of the surrounding area in the dim headlight beams of the car. The humid breeze felt like a warm blanket.

I checked into the resort and headed for my room. I may have slept on the plane but I was still jetlagged and emotionally exhausted. I wanted a hot bath and bed. The travel agent had told me I could stay a maximum of thirty days in the country without the need for a visa. That would allow plenty of time to explore this place.

Time to sleep.

***

I woke up with a jolt to realise someone was in my room. I stumbled out of bed.

"Room Service. Sorry, sorry, no scare, sorry," said a petite lady, her hands extended, shaking them from side to side.

"You sleep long; must eat." She pointed to the most amazing looking fruit platter I had ever seen.

"How long have I been asleep?"

"Maybe two day now," she said, shaking her head. "No good; must eat." She pointed to the fruit platter again.

I nodded. "Thank you."

The lady took one last look at the fruit platter and pointed to it as she walked out, closing the door behind her. I was in a complete daze. Had I really been asleep for two days? All I knew was that I was busting to pee. I rushed to the toilet and felt my body relax as the pressure on my bladder subsided. I jumped into the shower and brushed my teeth before sitting on the balcony with my wet hair in a towel bun and a towel around my body. I was ready to eat my breakfast.

***

On my way out to start my exploration I noticed that the phone on my bedside table had a red light flashing. I picked up the receiver and heard a voice recording say, "You have one message." I followed the prompts to retrieve the message. It was from Doug the travel agent. He wanted to ensure that I had arrived and that everything was to my liking. Great service, I thought to myself.

Walking through the streets of Phuket, I felt a sense of

familiarity, not of the place itself but rather the sensation of being in a foreign land. I loved seeing the signs in a language I could not read and the chaos of their manic road system. There was an untapped joy in my exploration that made me feel connected to my long-lost parents. This was a welcome surprise to the beginning of my journey.

I managed to find a series of markets that I weaved in and out of. There were piles of items stacked higher than was safe to reach. Clothes, shoes, pirated movies: the options were endless, and all for prices that were a slight on what would be charged in Australia. The scales of economy were so different in Thailand.

I eventually found myself out the front of a beauty house where massages were offered. The lady at the front was pointing to the price board and using hand gestures to encourage me to walk in. A thirty-minute massage came to the equivalent of five Australian dollars.

Just as I was about to walk inside, a voice came from behind and said, "The place up the road is cheaper."

I turned around to see Doug standing there.

"Hi," I said, an inquisitive expression on my face.

With a laugh, he responded, "I guess you weren't expecting to see me around these parts?"

"No, not really. What brings you to Thailand?"

He smiled and said with his arms spread out wide, "I was overdue for a holiday and being a travel agent has its perks. Free travel."

"You left me a message at the hotel. I picked it up this morning. I had no idea you were here. You never mentioned anything in the message."

"I know. I figured it was a small place and that I would bump into you."

"Hmm. Well, that you have."

I wanted to question him some more but knew better. If I asked, I might receive an answer that I wasn't ready for.

So I simply said, "Okay, where to from here?"

He had the biggest smile on his face. "I'll show you around all the hot spots in Phuket."

With that, Doug became my tour guide. He had been travelling to Thailand for the past six years, at least once a year, sometimes twice. His job did indeed afford him the luxury of travel and very cheap accommodation. Doug only had to commit to writing a positive review on the places he visited, adding some complimentary comments, and in return he received free or heavily discounted benefits. Nice.

We went to some amazing places to sample the cuisine. The amount of seafood and the variety that was on offer astounded me. Most of the sea creatures were still alive in tanks. You were expected to pick what you wanted slaughtered and point to the menu to show how you would like it prepared. It was rather barbaric to watch the excitement on the tourists' faces as they madly tapped on the window of the tank to point out their selected victim.

I had grown up on a working farm. I had witnessed Shane slaughtering his animals for meat and understood the process. Something stirred in me watching this tourist-driven spectacle. One majestic fish after another was pulled out and flapped around on the bench while the chef's assistant used the butt of his knife to deal a death blow to its head. Then with speed and admirable precision, he scaled and gutted the fish in preparation for cooking. I felt that there was no honour in the act of life sustaining life. It was in this place that I chose to become a vegetarian.

Thailand was where I learnt to appreciate a good old Aussie tradition: the pub-crawl. Doug and I went to almost every pub we could find. This statement is amusing to those who have been there before, because they will understand that there is a pub literally on every corner. In some places there are two, three and four. Hence, it didn't take very long to get pole-axed. We settled into a favourite haunt of Doug's that happened to be a Lady Bar. I naively assumed that meant it was a bar for ladies.

I even made a joke, warning that I was no lady and Doug cheekily snickered with the retort, "No worries; neither are they."

I'm pretty certain that he thought that I might freak out when I discovered the true meaning of Lady Boy. It didn't take me long to recognise that they were different. They were all dressed to the nines, had outstanding figures and their make-up was too perfect. I loved their polished look and sense of pride in their appearance.

I struck up a conversation with a few of them and before the night's end had a massive crowd of Lady Boys surrounding me, roaring with laughter. I had them exchanging stories about their experiences with customers, who paid them money in exchange for sexual favours. They eagerly showed me their parlour tricks to differentiate from one another. An example of this was when Lady Ruth lit up two cigarettes. She smoked one in her mouth and the other she placed in her pussy. I watched as she contracted her pelvic floor muscles to draw smoke in and then used the same muscles to release puffs of smoke. She even blew a smoke ring. Everyone clapped with vigour at each display of uniqueness. It was nice to feel their energy and experience their ability to allow joy into their otherwise challenged lives.

In the early hours of the next morning Doug walked me back to my hotel. The air was still and humid. I noted that there weren't too many wild animals lurking about, apart from the odd stray mangy dog and families of geckos. I joked that it was possibly because everything seemed to be on the menu. All the critters, great and small, were in hiding in constant fear of their lives. It was funny but also true.

I felt the awkward moment was upon us when Doug insisted on walking me to the door of my hotel room.

"I had an awesome time today, Doug. Thanks for finding me."

"Thank you. I thought I was taking you on an adventure. As it turns out, you indeed are the adventure. At every turn you managed to see things and engage people in ways I've never seen before. It was incredible."

"Thanks." I leaned in and gave him a light kiss on the cheek. I turned and said, "Good night," as I walked into my room.

The day had been exhilarating but my feet ached and I had an aroma of cigarette smoke, stale sweat and beer on my skin and clothes. I had a shower and hopped into bed to sleep.

***

A horrid noise invaded the room. I fumbled for the alarm. I couldn't seem to find the button to switch it off; in my stupor I realised it was the phone.

"Hello," I said in a husky voice.

"Morning. Breakfast finishes in thirty minutes. Rise and shine."

"Hey, Doug. What time is it?"

"Ten-thirty am. We got home at 3 am; plenty of sleep."

"For whom?"

"Come on, I want to take you to see some other stuff today."

"Okay – give me ten." I hung up and rested my head on the pillow. Cheez, he was a demanding creature. Who was that perky in the mornings?

As I drifted off to sleep, the phone started ringing again.

I answered, "Okay, okay, give me ten."

He laughed and hung up the phone.

I chuckled as I climbed out of bed and jumped into the shower. Pesky little creature, I thought to myself.

***

Doug was sitting in the foyer waiting for me. He pointed to a fruit platter. "I took the liberty of ordering you some breakfast."

I sat on the lounge across from him and started picking at the fruit. "What are the plans for today?"

"Glad you asked. I've decided that I'm not telling. It's going to be a surprise."

"What if I don't like surprises?"

"Talia, everyone likes surprises."

"I'm not like most people. I'm hard to read, rarely predictable and don't like surprises."

He laughed, shook his head and clapped his hands. "You have to pack a mini overnight bag. Finish your breakfast and I'll help you gather your things."

I intentionally ate my fruit incredibly slowly with a wicked smile on my face. He just laughed at me and assured me that he could wait. Eventually his foot started to tap. He bit his lower lip while looking anywhere except at me.

Finally Mr Patience jumped to attention. "Fuck it, come now or I'll carry you."

At first I didn't move but as he stepped closer I stretched out my arms as if to casually yawn and then confirmed that 'I' had finished breakfast.

"Are you sure, Talia?" he said with a smirk, stepping in closer.

"Yes, I've had an 'eloquent' sufficiency. Thanks for asking."

I could see that he enjoyed my cheeky behaviour; he walked behind me as I headed to my room. I could feel he was moving closer as we arrived at the door.

He placed his hands gently on my waist and whispered in my ear, "Careful or I might feel the need to spank you."

He squeezed his hands tighter around my waist as a warning before releasing me to enter the room. I was instantly turned on.

***

Bags packed, a short taxi ride and then we were on a substandard-looking watercraft they called a boat. It didn't look reliable, I couldn't see any emergency rafts and I was certain we were heading into shark-infested waters. I knew now that we were heading to Phi Phi Island for the full moon party. It was a manic festival that happened regularly in Thailand. I had seen brochures advertising this in the foyer of my hotel.

"How many of these parties have you been to before?"

"Heaps."

"So you survived the boat trip then?" I said, looking sheepishly over the edge into the dark waters.

He roared with laughter. "Yes, I survived."

I was glad when my feet again touched land. There had been moments when we were in the rough seas that I thought we would become sea fodder.

The beach was surprisingly crowded and the amount of people already stumbling around drunk was astounding. People from all walks of life were there to party and use the moon cycle as an excuse to become totally maggotted.

"Where are we going to stay?"

"No-one really organises a place to sleep at these parties. You just party and in the morning catch a boat back."

"Really?"

"Yep, backpackers do anything to save a dime."

"Let's just organise a room so we can safely leave our stuff. I'll pay."

"Talia, where's your sense of adventure? No hotels," he said, shaking his head. "Tonight we wing it."

"Fine," I said, rolling my eyes.

He grabbed my hand and took me to a special place on the island. It was set on a slight rise, a small hill, if you will, that allowed us to look back onto the mayhem taking place on the beach below.

"This is where we meet if we lose each other."

"Why would we lose each other?"

"We won't. It's just in case, okay?"

"Sure."

We left our belongings camouflaged under a nearby bush and headed back to the crowds to party. On the beach, in the heart of it all, the music was loud, the drinks were large and the crowds operated in waves and clusters. I knew after the first drink that I had already exceeded my alcohol limit. The organisers provided each person with a cup the size of a small bucket, filled with grog. I had no idea what was in that drink, but had my suspicions that it could fuel a rocket. The absence of street lighting made it a challenge to manoeuvre in between the swarm of people who were manically jumping around. I danced with random strangers, who would yell things up towards the moon, sticking their tongues out, bouncing and waving their hands. It was a mixture of amusing and disturbing to watch.

I loved getting lost in the manic atmosphere and enjoyed leaving it behind just as much. Slowly Doug and I made our way up towards the top of hill. In the darkness he reached his hand out to find mine. I liked it. We arrived at our special spot without the need to exchange a word. There is something to be said about being able to be in the presence of another and not feel the need to break the silence.

The moon that evening was captivating. It was so large and true in the sky. I turned to stand in front of Doug and leaned in to gently brush against his bottom lip. He instinctively went to take over and kiss me.

I moved my head back, placed my hands on his face and said, "Shhh."

He stood still as I leaned in close and explored his top lip. I licked the outline of his mouth and then gently chewed his bottom lip and tugged. Once again Doug tried to take over.

I pulled back, smiled as I shook my head. "Shhh."

His stare was intense as he watched me trace the outline of his face, across the tip of his nose, around his lips, down to his chin. I traced my finger down his neck and kissed his Adam's apple. I unbuttoned his white linen shirt slowly as I stared into his eyes and bit my bottom lip in anticipation of what was to come.

As I leant in to kiss his nipples, he reached across and started to play with the cheeks of my arse. I could feel his intensity rise as he lifted my face and started to kiss me with the voraciousness of a hungry beast. He pressed his erection up against me and ripped at my T-shirt to wrench it off my body. He unclasped my bra and turned me around to face the moon. His hands kneaded at my breasts while he kissed my neck.

I reached behind and rubbed against his jeans and whispered, "Take them off."

We both removed the remainder of our clothes and I turned back to the position that I could see was his pleasure pulse. I knelt down first on my knees and then on all fours.

"Oh, Talia," he said as he ran his hand up the arch of my back to my neck then back down again, skimming the outer edge of my buttocks all the way to my toes. He gently separated my legs, got on all fours and placed his face directly onto my hot pulsating vagina. Doug had clearly done this before. He expertly stimulated my clitoris with varying intensity. He alternated his hands to reach from underneath my torso to squeeze and pull at my nipples. I was incredibly turned on. I found myself uninhibited and grinding against his face, panting.

He grabbed the cheeks of my arse to steady my zealous pumping. I wanted to ride that glorious pleasure pony down the home straight and then some. I dropped my torso lower to the ground so that I could reach across to play with myself. Watching me masturbate sent Doug into overdrive. He rose to his knees and positioned his body; with no mercy he plunged deep inside me and pulled out again just as quickly. Over and over he did this, sending electric pulsating signals through my core.

I arched my back and lifted my chin towards the sky to amplify the intensity. He tugged at my hair, slapped my arse and made grunting noises as he increased his speed. It was intense. It did not take me long before my fingers were clawing at the dirt and I was convulsing so hard that I thought that the earth was moving beneath me. Doug climaxed hard and fast soon after my body surrendered to its own shuddery delight. Panting with shortened breath, I laid my head on my arms, saying, "Oh, my God."

Passion

The next couple of days went by quickly, with Doug and I consuming our time sightseeing and fucking in the great outdoors. There was a heightened sense of excitement to the act when sex was in an environment where we both were exposed to the elements and the possibility of being caught.

On Doug's last night in Thailand we went out for dinner, then he took me to my first-ever open-air martial arts tournament. It was a full contact Muay Thai Kickboxing Championship match. He bribed a man to arrange us a row behind the ringside seats, so we were close enough to hear the crunching of bone and to get splattered with their sweat, blood and tears.

The pre-match fights consisted of kids as young as ten with six-pack abs engaging in full contact fighting. It was brutal. The crowd cheered the winners and threw anything they had in reach at the losers. Initially I wanted to lurch forward to shield the loser in protest at the crowd's behaviour. After the third match I was acclimatised to the environment and had less of an emotional bind.

The main event was actually amazing to watch. I found a level of personal acceptance in watching two grown men choosing to beat each other. It was a title fight so one was hungry to retain the title while the other was trying to win it. Unlike the kids, these guys demonstrated fantastic technique and stamina. Their speed and ability to pre-empt one another's strikes indicated that they were well matched. I found myself lost in the moment. I shifted in my chair and threw pre-emptive blocks and air punches.

On the way back to the hotel I jumped about and re-enacted the final blows of the knock-out.

"Talia."

Still bouncing around and throwing air punches, I responded, "Doug."

"You know I'm leaving tomorrow."

"Actually today; it's just after midnight."

He stopped walking. "Talia, can you desist with the bouncing around for a second?"

I glanced across and could see the look. I stopped bouncing.

"I'm leaving today and you don't seem to mind."

"You told me at the beginning that you were only here for six days, so I already knew that there was a time limit."

He closed his eyes and paused for a second. "Talia, I really like you. I didn't just happen to be going to Thailand. I booked my ticket and took the time off straight after I met you. I caught the very next flight out. I was drawn to you. I wanted us to happen."

There was a long pause before I responded, "I know." I watched an expression of disbelief spread across his brow.

"You knew? How?"

"It was strange that you didn't tell me at the time that I booked my flight that you were heading there too, so I concluded that you chose to make plans after I walked out the door. To add to this, when you found me outside the beauty salon, I didn't feel like it was an accident. You were relieved that you had located me and excited when I agreed to hang out."

"That's very perceptive. What else do you think you know?"

"I don't want to play this game, Doug. Come on, we had a great few days. Can we not do this? Please?"

"It's not a game. I'm just curious."

"Okay, you told me that you were already in Thailand when you left me the message. I had originally thought that I'd been here a couple of days before you arrived, but then I saw the fruit platter that you ordered for me the morning after we had bumped into each other. The housekeeper who came into my room had provided me with the same fruit platter. I realised that it was more likely that you had booked a room in the same hotel and were waiting for me. When I didn't surface, you placed a courtesy call, hoping I would answer. When that produced no results, you got room service to check on me and provide me with a complimentary breakfast fruit platter. Close enough?"

"So you knew this whole time that I'd done all of this and you never said a word?"

"I had my suspicions, but I saw no point in validating it."

"Wow, no point?" He let out a laugh that held no humour. "Stupid, stupid me," he said, shaking his head and kicking some stones on the ground. "In my mind I had this foolish romantic idea that I would surprise you with how I felt when I first laid eyes on you. I wanted you to swoon, melting into my arms when I revealed that I was driven to cross an ocean to pursue you."

"Can we stop this now? I'm not going to feel guilty for allowing myself to enjoy your company. You offered to be with me and I accepted. I don't regret that. I WON'T regret that."

He stood with his hands deep in his pockets, staring at the ground and shaking his head. Six days into my escape and I had managed to create the Ethan scenario all over again. I stood there because I honestly didn't know what else to do. Eventually he started walking towards the hotel and I silently walked beside him. I had mixed emotions about it all. I felt like a heel watching him yearn for more. Perhaps I had a heart of rubber and these interludes were trying their best to penetrate the surface, only the harder they tried the further they bounced. I wanted to hold steadfast to being myself. He was fun; I liked him but I didn't want to be in a relationship with him.

When we arrived at the hotel he stopped in the foyer. He didn't look at me. He kept his head low and I could see him drawing shallow breaths. I knew that he was trying to hold back tears driven by frustration.

In a barely audible voice he spoke. "If it's okay with you, I want to keep it casual and say goodbye now. I don't want to have this false hope that you will change your mind."

He paused to give me an opportunity to interject.

I didn't.

He let out a sigh. "I feel like a right fool at the moment."

His hands were still tucked deep in his jeans pockets when I walked across and put my arms around him.

"Safe travels," was all I could think to say.

He reacted to this by swinging his body to fling my arms off him and stormed away, heading towards his room mumbling some words and then yelling an elongated, "FUUUUUuuck," so loud that it echoed through the corridors.

The cleaning lady was across the way in the shadows staring at me. I shrugged my shoulders and shook my head to acknowledge her presence. She jumped when she heard Doug's door slam. In a scurry, she recommenced her work.

Back in my room, I had a hot shower to wash away the essence of what had happened. I decided that when I turned off the water that was to be the end of my thought allowance for this event. There was nothing that I could do or say to make him feel better, so this had to be his journey not mine. I lay in my bed staring out the window at the night sky and drifted off to sleep.

***

When I woke the first thing I saw was the red flashing button on my hotel phone. It was 10 am. If Doug maintained his planned course, he should be in a taxi on the way to the airport. I dressed and headed out for a wander around the streets of Thailand. It was amazing how the same paths we had walked presented differently in his absence. Everything new again. There was nothing to distract me, so I tuned into my surroundings, allowing myself to feel connected.

I gravitated down a street that was foreign to me, some way from the main stretch of town. There was a déjà vu moment that cloaked my mind when I saw a lady sweeping her front porch. She looked at me and smiled knowingly. There was a familiarity about her, yet I was certain I had not laid eyes on her before. Perhaps I had seen her subconsciously while walking through the markets. It was a surreal moment that had no known meaning to me. I kept walking down the path until I could see a rice paddy ahead.

That was the end of the road, I thought to myself as I walked to its very edge.

Swarms of dragonflies hovered above the rice reeds, the water providing the perfect breeding ground for them to flourish. Perhaps this was their nursery. I crouched down and watched. It was spectacular to witness their dance across the surface of the glistening water. Some of the larger dragonflies' wings released multicoloured hues as light beamed through their wings. It must have been the position of the sunlight in moments that produced this glorious event. It seemed as though I was witnessing something that only they were otherwise privy to.

I jumped to attention when I felt a hand placed on my shoulder. I had not heard any footsteps so I was completely startled and my heart pounded as I spun to see the old lady.

"You scared me," I said, placing my hand on my chest and mimicking my heart pounding.

She put her hand over her mouth and chuckled. Using her other hand, she pointed behind me. I turned back to the rice paddy. Following the direction of her bony finger, I saw a man waving in the distance. I raised my hand and waved back.

How strange, I thought to myself.

The other side of the paddy field looked like a forest or an overgrown swamp of some sort. I had been so fixated on what was before me that I hadn't paid any attention to the place beyond the paddy. I could see now that there was a curl of smoke rising from what I assumed was a chimney. As I gazed upon the man once more, I now saw that he was gesturing me to come forward. I looked at the water before me.

The old lady brushed past me as she leaped forward into the paddy. There was a small splash but her feet seemed to stay on the surface of the water. *How was that possible?* She continued to walk forward and used her hand to gesture that I should follow. In an unexpected moment, I leaped forward into the paddy as the woman had done and found myself walking on water. In actuality it was a raised platform that had been built just below the surface of the water line. I couldn't see it from where we had been standing and it was not built all the way to the edge of the field. I gather that was done on purpose to provide the illusion of the end of something when in fact it was just the beginning.

When I reached the other side, the man was no longer there. The old lady stood waiting with her hands clasped and a welcoming smile. As my first foot touched the earth, she bowed and turned to walk down a path shaded by a canopy of trees. The first thing I noticed was how cool it was. The second and the most delightful thing was the transition from what seemed to be tropical foliage to a bamboo forest. There was an amazing energy to this space and I felt honoured to be there. It never once crossed my mind to be scared.

When we arrived at a clearing I saw a couple of large open huts and I could see part of a smaller one set behind. I sat on the edge of the porch of the main hut and looked across at the path from where I had just come. This was a reconfirmation in my mind that all is never what it seems. Possessing new eyes brought new perspective. Instinctually I felt that I needed to be here.

The old man came out and gave me a cup with something in it. I smelt it and then drank down the fresh coconut milk. He stood waiting for the cup to be returned and then gestured that he could provide me more. I smiled and shook my head. It was obvious now that neither of them spoke much English, if at all. This was perfect. Words complicated communication. People were not able to hear the intent of a message that was passed when they were clouded by their own thoughts, desires, fears and judgement.

When they both came out again I could see now that they were a couple.

I stood to face them and said, "Talia," patting my hand on my chest.

They nodded in acknowledgement and the old man said, "Boon," tapping at himself and "Pom," tapping at his lovely lady, who smiled and nodded in agreement.

Boon then said something to her and walked inside the hut.

Pom jumped off the edge of the porch and said, "Taha," gesturing with her hand that I should follow.

I smiled at her pronunciation of my name and felt no need to correct it. In this place I would be Taha. Pom took me to the smaller hut at the back. Inside it was one large room that had a hammock in a corner with some netting around it. Each of the sides of the hut had a window with a stick holding the shutter ajar. It was rudimentary with less than the basics I was accustomed to.

I surveyed the room, noting the absence of a toilet. Pom laughed. As if she could read my thoughts, she grabbed my hand and took me to the back window. She lifted the shutter higher so we could have a clear view out to the back forest. She pointed out to the bushes and then down to the ground on the outside of the hut where there was a bucket with some water. Looking at me again, she nodded, waiting for an acknowledgment that I understood. I nodded with a smile.

Boon called out and Pom once again walked off, saying, *"Taha mā."*

I assumed this meant that I needed to follow.

This time we walked onto the back porch and through the back entrance. I could smell the aroma of spices and hear the sizzling of a pan. The hut had a sense of enormity on the inside that needed to be appreciated. The walls were high and the detail in the weave of the raw material protecting us from the elements was visually perfect.

"Boon," she said, pointing to the space and smiling proudly.

"Boon?" I said, touching the wall and stretching up towards the direction of the ceiling.

"Chì Boon."

Boon entered the room and smiled. He looked around the room and with a beaming smile reconfirmed the words, "Chì Boon."

I clapped my hands and nodded my head. "Very good."

They sat me down to have lunch with them. There was no ceremony to eating there; they served me up some of the food in a bowl then without hesitation proceeded to eat theirs. I noticed that they glanced at one another when I took my first mouthful. I recognised immediately that they were expecting that the food might be too spicy for me to consume. I had known when I first entered the room with the infusion of smells that they were not shy with their use of chillies. Luckily for me, I had sensory deprivation from years of eating super-hot foods. Shane and Ruth's food for the most part was bland, but I had always managed to add some chilli jam or other spicy concoction into the mix to make it worthy of my mouth. I loved rich flavours. Boon and Pom seemed pleased at my non-reaction to their spicy cuisine.

After lunch Pom headed back down the path towards the rice paddy. Boon gestured for me to follow him and we headed off in the other direction. Deep in the forest he picked out various leaves and said something, encouraging me to smell them, touch them and, in some cases, taste them. He would pretend to choke himself to indicate vegetation that was poisonous. It was fascinating to find that an ordinary leaf that I would have overlooked, when chewed, released an explosion of spearmint flavour, and yet the tree that delivered the visually tempting bouquet of low-hanging purple fruits was not to be touched.

Boon enjoyed showcasing his knowledge of the forest that surrounded him. I felt honoured that he was taking the time to share this with me.

In the afternoon, as the sun amplified it's release of heat, Boon jumped on his hammock and signalled for me to go to the hut, no doubt to do the same. I didn't tend to sleep much as a general rule, yet in this space I felt so relaxed I believed that a nanna nap could be achieved. The laughable part was underestimating the skill of climbing into a hammock. Boon seemed to leap in. My attempt was successful but a lot less elegant. When I finally got into a comfortable position where I didn't fear that I was going to fall out, I drifted off to sleep as the hammock gently swayed from side to side.

A couple of hours later I woke to be greeted by the mosquito netting full of starving little blighters. Hundreds of them were spread across the netting, watching, waiting for their moment. I reached into my day bag and brought out the good old Aussie staple, Aeroguard Tropical Strength. There was no way I was leaving this space without ensuring they were dead or at least on the brink. I coated myself in a lather of the spray as well as saturating the netting before walking out from underneath the veil to head towards the main hut.

At the front of the hut I saw Boon doing a rhythmical series of movements. He didn't seem to notice me at all. I quietly propped myself on the edge of the porch, leaning against a supporting post to watch. One movement flowed into another. I guessed that he was doing some form of Tai Chi.

Boon was not a tall man. I am five foot seven inches, so I assumed that he was about five foot five inches. Although his face was weathered from lengthy exposure to the elements, he still had the beautiful Thai complexion and healthy glow to his skin. The outline of his torso under his baggy clothing made me think that he had little fat on his body; it was all muscle and sinew. The elasticity in his movements was impressive. One minute his right leg was in a crouching position with his knee pointed out the side while the other leg stretched low to the ground as in a partial split. In a swing of his arms he would swoop forward and leap to the sky, higher than I imagined possible from that position.

Upon completion of the workout, Boon walked straight over to me. Smiling, he tapped my legs and swung them round so they were hanging off the edge of the porch. He gestured for me to jump to the ground.

I stood before him. He looked into my eyes as his hand reached out to place two fingers on the centre of my breastbone. He tapped twice and left his fingers pressed in position on my chest. The other hand rose and tapped on the centre of my forehead just above the bridge of my nose. He tapped twice and pressed in again hard before releasing. Boon then grabbed my right hand and placed it in a single-hand praying position against my breastbone. My other hand was placed in a praying position against my forehead. He gestured for me to hold the position with strength. Boon took a couple of steps back and placed his own hands in the same position and then demonstrated what he wanted me to do.

Pom appeared, smiling with approval at my attempts to execute what Boon was patiently showing me. She went inside the hut to cook dinner while we continued. I had sweat pouring off my body and the salty water from my brow trickled into my eyes, causing my vision to blur. The light sting of the salt caused me to squint. I must have looked a right treat, for when Pom resurfaced from her cooking duties she released laughter and a series of snorts that made both Boon and I join in.

Thankfully the lesson was over.

The movements he had taught me were slow, controlled. It was the stillness that surprisingly caused my muscles to burn. Doing nothing was exhausting, so by its nature I must be doing something.

We went inside to eat. I found it a struggle to sit on the floor in any particular position for long and Boon noticed. I watched him watching me and knew that he was devising his next lesson.

After dinner we all sat for a while in silence on the porch.

I eventually stood up and gave a slight head bow. "Good night."

They both said, *"rātrī s̄ was̄ di,"* as I disappeared around the corner.

I hopped into my hammock and managed for the first time in what seemed like forever to get a good night's sleep.

***

In the morning I felt energised. Dawn was breaking, so small streams of light were coming through one of windows, a welcome light breeze drifted in and those pesky mosquitoes were still for the most part trapped on the outside of the netting. I had a couple of bites; nothing, really, compared to the looming threat of the hundreds of hungry little suckers waiting to pounce. I sprayed my surrounds and myself and headed out the door.

My guess was that it was just after 6 am. My natural cycle was to sleep late and rise early. It was only when I felt unwell or was sad that I managed to conjure up the need to sleep forever. As a general rule I never wore a watch. I had always felt that the restriction of twenty-four hours as a count of time was not necessary. It was a concept born of man and his need for the illusion of control and conformity. I believed in the notion of past, present, future and that time does elapse. It was more the confines of the twenty-four hours that I disliked.

I could feel nature calling. This was going to be interesting. I collected my bucket and traipsed into the jungle with only the early streams of dawn light dancing through the canopy of leaves to light the way. I found a clearing, dropped my dacks and crouched down. I hadn't quite thought this through. Balancing while pushing proved to be challenging. When I had finished, I used some wide heart-shaped leaves, which I folded into more manageable sections, to wipe myself clean. I poured some water on my hands to wash them. Job done.

Before heading back, I gathered more of the leaves in case I needed to go again. I wasn't keen on coming back to the same spot every time, so I thought it prudent to get some supplies.

The others were still sleeping so I headed back to the rice paddy. I sat at the edge of the waters and watched the way the sun rose across the sky. It was going to be another scorching day. I sat and watched the dragonflies until I heard my hosts calling my name. When I arrived back at the huts, I was greeted with a big cuddle from both of them. I took it as a sign that they were glad I was still there.

Pom left after we had eaten breakfast together. She went down the path towards the rice paddy. Boon gestured for me to join him in some morning Tai Chi. We stood facing each other. He executed the movements and I tried as best I could to mimic them. I was captivated by his ability to stare past me; I wanted to reach that space. After thirty minutes he was finished his well-oiled routine. He re-connected with my eyes and with no hesitation he assumed his role as the teacher again.

After lunch, instead of going for the walk with Boon, I gestured that I was heading down the path towards the paddies. I tried as best I could to explain that I would come back. They seemed to acknowledge my fumbled gestures so I headed out the way I had come. It was only in the absence of access to a westernised bathroom that I realised how comforting it was to have one nearby. When I walked into my hotel room I could see a note had been placed on my bed. I knew it was from Doug. Who else could it be?

I jumped in the shower, welcoming the release from my sweat-, dust- and Areoguard-clogged pores. There was such sweet relief in water freely falling on my body; I could have stayed there for hours. I brushed my teeth, managed to comb most of the dreads out of my hair and then felt ready to receive the message. It was only when I sat down that I realised that it was a letter addressed to me, posted to this hotel.

Inside was a lengthy letter from Ethan. He had written three A4 size pages back and front on how he felt about me, how he felt about the way I had left, the words I had written in my note. His words evoked great sadness in me. I knew that I was never going to be able to fulfill his desires for long-term commitment; I simply didn't feel the depth he felt. There were moments where I had felt intensity of love for him, but I was never in love with him. In the letter he said that I was everything to him.

I went into the bathroom, took a match to the letter and envelope and let it burn in the sink. I stared into the eyes of my refection in the mirror until my surroundings blurred out of sight. I inhaled the smoke rising from the flames, whispering the words for the wind to carry into his dreams ,"You are not all of everything to me. Seek another." I washed the last of the ashes from the sink, wishing them and him well on their journey.

I had no idea how he had managed to track me down. I hadn't even known that I was heading to Thailand until I arrived at the airport. I guess that how he found me didn't matter; he knew where I was and had written his letter of what I hoped would be a form of closure for him.

I grabbed my things and headed for the door. Just before I walked out I remembered that I was not done. I took a deep breath and turned to greet the flashing red light on the phone. I dialled in the code and listened to the ten messages Doug had left me. It was a rollercoaster ride ranging from apologies to anger to crying then anger again and finishing on an apology. I deleted the last of the voicemails and headed out the door.

At the desk downstairs I explained to the concierge that I was going to be travelling a little and that I would not require room service. My original intention had been to release my room booking but the lure of having access to a shower and flushing toilet was too great. I wasn't quite ready to give them up. Even if I never came back to the hotel, just the thought of knowing that I had access to my room in an emergency was enough for now.

On my way back to the paddy fields I entered a small supermarket of sorts. I bought the key essentials: twenty rolls of toilet paper and as much bottled water as I could carry. As I walked back down the street that ended at the rice paddy, I saw Pom at the same house again. This time she was washing windows.

I called out, "Hello, Pom."

She turned to greet my call with an eager wave and big smile. She had a lovely energy about her.

I crossed the rice field, walked down the path through the majestic bamboo forest and into the clearing. Boom leaped out of his hammock, calling out my Thai name, Taha, and came to my side to assist me with my load. When he saw the rolls of toilet paper he laughed with vigour. I laughed at him laughing at me.

He stopped laughing when he saw my big beautiful heart-shaped leaves on my porch. He pointed to them and then pointed at me. I nodded and reached down to pick one up. Quick as a viper's strike, he blocked my hand and pushed it away with an expression that warned that I should not touch the leaves. He grabbed my hands and inspected them closely. After a while he looked at me with curiosity and pointed to the leaves again while stroking the palm of my hand. I grabbed a toilet roll and tore off a couple of sheets. Then, pointing to the leaves, I showed him how I had folded the leaf and then used it to wipe.

He grabbed a stick and flipped over one of the leaves to reveal a pale underside. He tapped on the pale side and pointed and then tapped on the dark green side of the other leaf and pointed. I took the stick and tapped the dark green side. At this he burst out laughing, slapped his leg and laughed until he couldn't anymore. He had tears streaming down his face.

He could see that I didn't quite appreciate how hilarious the situation was, so he lifted his hands to gesture he would be back. He ran inside and came out just as quickly with a clump of goop on a leaf. Picking up the stick again, he rubbed the pale side of the leaf and without a word of warning wiped a small portion of its secretion across my left arm just above my wrist. In seconds I could feel a burning sensation similar to that of stinging nettles. My skin was alive with a growing intensity of pain. A red welt appeared before my eyes as my skin started to blister.

Boon placed the leaf with the goop on my wound and held his hand there for applied pressure. It was immediately soothing. Soon the sting ceased. He looked at me and smiled. I nodded my head: I got it. He once again burst into laughter and this time so did I. Disaster averted by pure arse luck. Literally!

***

That night over dinner Boon explained what happened to Pom. He even did a little re-enactment of my explanation, elongating his words to describe his line of questioning. It had almost transformed into a one person play as he jumped from one side to another to delineate between my character and his. He was quite the storyteller, it would seem. That night we all roared with laughter until our bellies hurt. It looked like I was going to be the butt of all the jokes from here on. I didn't mind. It seemed as though they needed to have more joy in their lives and in this moment I loved being the one able to provide them with what they needed.

***

Over the next couple of weeks we developed a routine. In the morning I would rise, practise my Tai Chi, have breakfast and then do a synchronised Tai Chi routine with Boon. Once this was complete he would show me new moves, blocks, punches, kicking techniques. In the afternoon he would spar with me. At first he did everything in slow motion, then the next pass would be faster and so the momentum would continue until I could not keep up anymore.

Initially I didn't realise during the spar sessions that it would be slap contact. He was trying to demonstrate that in order for me to know and pre-empt a person I only needed to watch their eyes. If I focused on the part that moved I would be distracted and not able to see anything else. After a multitude of whacks across the arms, legs, head and torso I managed to see the distinct advantage to his technique of positioning and observation. We would work out to the point of exhaustion. It was exhilarating.

In the late afternoons when Boon took his nap I would head into town to take a shower and get a massage. I didn't want to have muscle soreness as my excuse not to work out so the lady in the shop would rub a pungent cocktail of herbs infused in oil onto my skin. The oil would penetrate deep into my muscles. I'm not sure what was in that concoction. All I knew was that it worked. I felt invincible.

On my last night that I planned to be with them I noticed upon my return from the masseuse that there was an extra hammock hanging on the porch of the front hut. Boon called out to someone as he saw me arrive. A guy appeared on the porch and behind him was Pom.

"Hello," I said, as I got closer to where they were standing.

The boy jumped off the porch and with a confident stride walked up to greet me. "Hi, I'm Siam, their son. You can call me Zee."

I put my hand out as a gesture to shake his hand; he smiled and shook my hand.

"You speak English really well. How is it that your parents don't speak any?"

He laughed. "Based on what my father has told me so far, you have all managed to find a way to communicate just fine."

I smiled. "Indeed."

"Come inside. Mum has cooked a feast tonight in honour of us meeting."

I walked inside, blown away by how she had transformed the open space with lanterns lit everywhere. Fresh flower petals were scattered on the floor and a lovely smell of perfume wafted in the air.

"Zee, please let her know that I think it's beautiful."

He translated for me and Pom responded, saying that he didn't need to tell her what my face already did.

We ate dinner and once again laughed until our bellies could not cope any more. Zee's presence offered me an opportunity to tell them some of my interpretations of the experiences I had had since my arrival. It was a spectacular evening of joy.

Later, after our meal had settled, Boon asked me to join him to display to his son the Tai Chi routine he had taught me. We were like a well-oiled machine. I had done these moves a thousand times across the last twenty days. I could feel the interconnected energy of each of the moves, as it was series of circular patterns that fused into one for me.

Upon completion, Boon said something to Zee, gesturing to me. Zee shook his head. In a stern voice, Boon repeated the words. Zee hopped off the porch, walked across and stood in front of me.

"My father wants me to fight you."

I looked at Boon, who nodded to assure me that it was okay.

I shrugged. "Okay. I'm only learning, so be gentle," I said with a smile and then took my position.

Zee glanced one more time at his father and then started with a medium-speed hand strike towards my left temple. I didn't flinch. I saw the move and automatically pulled my head back to dodge the blow. Using my hand to encourage the momentum of his hand in the direction past my head, I slapped him in the midriff with my free hand. I could see that Zee was a little shocked by my successful strike and in his mind was quickly deciding to no longer be kind to me. Each time he made a move I was able at speed to counterattack and slap him. Boon stopped the display when he could see that Zee was starting to get agitated.

Boon said something to Zee that made his expression change to disbelief.

"You have only been training for three weeks?"

"Yes, with your dad."

He looked at his dad and nodded. Then he turned to me and bowed. "You have a gift," he said.

"I think it's more likely that you father is a great teacher."

"Taha, you are fast. Your ability to pre-empt my moves and your timing is very good. Father says you have the mind of a warrior. Embrace your gift."

I didn't want to debate this. It was a lovely compliment. I stood before Boon and placed a single hand in the prayer position on my forehead and one on my chest as he had shown me. I shifted the lower hand up and the other down so that they met together in a prayer state in front of my mouth. Boon then did the same, saying something to Zee.

"Father says that you started with your head and your heart in two spaces when you came here. Now you are able to put them together. With discipline and practice, you will be able to unite them to find the peace you need."

I mouthed the words 'thank you' to Boon and Pom. They smiled and walked inside.

As I positioned myself to sit on the porch, Zee did the same.

"My name isn't Taha, it's Talia. Your parents didn't pronounce my name right and I never corrected them."

Zee laughed. "My parents intentionally called you Taha. That is an unspoken compliment. They instantly gave you a name that the evil spirits would not know and therefore could not use to lure you away. It is an old Thai belief. That is why most people use their nicknames rather than their birth names."

"Ha. Funny. This is another example where it reconfirms that nothing is ever what it seems. If I hadn't told you my real name, I never would have known the truth behind Taha."

"I could tell you something else," said Zee with a tease in his voice.

"Go on."

"I was shocked to learn that they had taken a foreigner into our home. This is not something they have ever done. If I hadn't seen it with my own eyes I wouldn't have believed it."

"I thought this was something that they did on occasion for tourist money."

"Never," he said. "Never ever," he insisted as if to drive home a point that was already crystal.

"Why did they choose to take me in?"

Zee looked across at me. "Mother insists that when she saw you walking down the street that she recognised your soul. She believes that she has been your mother in another life. Dad too felt something and wanted you to come. It is strange."

I could feel myself becoming overwhelmed with an intensity of emotion that I had not felt in the longest time. I hadn't expected him to say that. I looked at him with tears freefalling down my cheeks.

"What is it, Taha?"

"I felt that she was familiar to me too. I thought I was

experiencing some déjà vu when I saw her sweeping the porch. The time spent here has been amazing. I really feel blessed for the experience, but most of all, for the first time in forever I feel the loss of my own parents with a gravity that I cannot bear to have surface."

I sobbed, using my hands to cover my face. I couldn't stop the tears but I could hide from him the anguish on my face.

Zee sat in silence while I cried. The only words he spoke were, "I am sorry, Taha." Then he shifted across to put his arm around me.

"They died when I was six, drowned. I never really knew them." I looked across to greet Zee's gaze. "I have never told anyone that before."

I wiped the remaining tears from my face and jumped off the porch. Turning to Zee, I half-smiled. "I'm going to get some sleep."

"Goodnight, Taha."

Before I turned the corner, I spoke into the darkness. "Zee."

"Yes."

"Will you be here in the morning when I wake?"

"Yes."

"Good. I plan to leave in the morning. I want to say goodbye to your parents and would like you to translate for me."

"Are you leaving because of what I told you?"

"No. I was always planning to leave tomorrow. I have two more days before my flight. It leaves from Bangkok, so I'm catching a flight across there tomorrow afternoon. Goodnight."

"Night."

***

In the morning I felt the sobering reality that I was leaving this place. The whole family was waiting for me on the porch. I suspected by the look on their faces that Zee had already told them that I was leaving. I smiled and opened my arms to Pom. She gladly entered into my embrace. I looked at Zee and said what he needed to interpret for me.

"I feel honoured to have had you recognise me in another form and another life. Blessed is the mother that loves her children through space and time. The depth of your connection will never be forgotten and will always be cherished by me."

She squeezed me tightly as the words were translated. We all had tears flowing freely. As she stepped back her hand stroked my face. She had such soft hands for a woman who worked so hard.

I walked over to Boon, placed my right hand across his forehead and the other diagonally on his chest across his heart. I gazed deep into his eyes and said, "Your generosity of time and teaching has evoked a passion in me that will never again sleep. I will always feel forever grateful for you unlocking what I didn't know existed. When I arrived I felt strong of mind, now I leave feeling the growing strength of heart. Thank you." I placed my head on his forehead and then took two steps back to execute the praying-hand gesture and a bow.

I jumped off the porch and took an envelope from my bag. I passed it across to Pom with a smile.

"Zee, please translate this one last thing for me."

He nodded.

"This is a small token of my thanks and blessings.

Please accept this with no offence and open it when I leave."

I pulled out the last of the toilet paper and left it on the porch with a cheeky smile. They all laughed. I grabbed my things and walked down the path once more towards the rice fields. I raised my hand to wave, not looking back, knowing that they were watching. It was time to go.

As I reached the other side of the rice paddy, I heard Zee calling out to me. I turned and saw him coming out from the forest and across the paddy field.

Out of breath, he stammered, "We cannot take this money."

"It would be an insult not to," I said, pushing his arm with the envelope back to his chest. "Zee, I never expected to receive so much from choosing to walk down this street and into a rice paddy field. Please give this money to your parents and tell them to enjoy their lives."

"Thank you. It will change everything."

"They never have to worry about providing food on the table again. Perhaps they could volunteer to adopt an orphan child? Start teaching Tai Chi to people who need to connect with something? They both have so much to offer. This is theirs to spend as they choose."

"Thank you, Taha. They will never forget you. I will never forget you."

"Nice to meet you, Zee." I grabbed my things and walked down towards the main street.

Cause and Effect

On my return trip, I stopped over in Hong Kong to look around for a few days. It was a fast-moving place with manic design. I arranged a private tour of the network of underground homes built between the buildings. It was not a space that many non-residents were allowed to access, which made it all the more intriguing to explore.

I stood out like a sore thumb as we wandered the dark narrow enclave. There were electrical wires everywhere, on the ground and above our heads. It was a tangled mass that looked like the network of veins in the human body. This space seemed like an endless labyrinth that was fascinating to explore. I walked the dimly lit narrow paths, listening to layers of voices, TVs and radios all in a fusion of noise.

I was moved when I saw a lady sitting on a crate in a room that had dirty water running down the wall. She was breast-feeding her baby while rocking back and forth, saying something to her child in a soothing tone. I came out of that experience appreciating that love could exist anywhere.

I am yet to understand why street merchants seemed fixated on selling me items that were targeted for aphrodisiac enhancement. Snake bile, tiger penis and swallow saliva were hot ticket items. The man with the snake bile followed me for three blocks, waving a fly-ridden thing near my face, repeating the words, "Good medicine, good for you, good for you," over and over. Eventually a passerby told him to go away. When I asked him what he was trying to sell me, he told me that it was the shit sack of a snake that's supposed to increase love potency.

Fuck me, that's the last thing I need, I thought to myself.

I joined a group tour arranged by the hotel where I was staying. It entailed a full day of looking at the local famous sites, which included a visit to Lantau Island to climb to the Po Lin Monastery. I wanted to rub the tummy of the famous big Buddha.

The man sitting next to me was a businessman from Tel Aviv called Yigal. It was his first time in Hong Kong so he had decided to take a day off to take a look around. The company that he represented specialised in manufacturing computer hardware components. Yigal had been married by arrangement when he was in his late teens, was forty-four years of age and had three children. This was his first time travelling to a foreign country. I assured him this was going to be an experience he would never forget.

The first stop was the famous fresh food markets. We walked through a dimly lit space and saw all kinds of animals squashed into cages, boxes, crates, still alive and hoping not to be chosen. The place stank with mottled aromas that contradicted the notion of 'fresh'. We witnessed heads chopped off chickens, eels whacked with the butt of a knife.

I turned to Yigal, who was using his hand to block his nose, and said, "I get it now."

"Get what?" he said, while struggling to breathe through his mouth.

"I understand why this place smells so bad."

"Why?"

"Because the animals are all shitting themselves knowing their fate."

We both laughed but knew there was an essence of truth to it.

***

Lunch was served after we had climbed the steps to Po Lin Monastery. The monks put on a vegetarian spread. In the centre of the table was a big golden turkey made of a fake primarily tofu meat flavoured to simulate turkey. I cringed at the idea of eating something that was synthesised to look and taste like the real thing. What was the point of that? I stuck to eating the veggies and watched in amazement as others, including the monks, took slices of the fake meat. It made me wonder why they would pretend to eat something that their religion promoted not to touch. To me this was symbolic of the pretence that co-exists in one's life.

After lunch, the tour guide suggested that people look around and reconvene in an hour.

I looked at Yigal and with a cheeky smile said, "If I lead, are you willing to follow?"

He smiled, shook his head but reluctantly said, "Yes."

I laughed and headed off in the direction of drums I

could hear in the distance. We found a group of young children hitting drums and singing a tune. I danced around them with my arms open and joined in the chanting on the pieces that were repetitive and becoming familiar. Their singing became louder as they joined hands to form a circle with me. They followed my lead and would lift their hands in the air, step into the circle, then step back, repeating this over and over while the singing continued. I indicated to Yigal that he should join in. Much to my surprise, he did. Crowds formed to watch the spectacle. When the song was done, I clapped and waved my hands at the kids. They surrounded me, clambering for a cuddle. It was delightful.

Next stop I saw a sign that said 'do not enter'. I looked at Yigal for a moment and then turned to walk into the space that was forbidden. Prying open a large ornate wooden door, I found I was now standing inside a private prayer room in the monastery. The columns that held up the enormous structure were over five metres in circumference. The majesty of the architecture was breathtaking. Yigal couldn't resist and followed me into the forbidden space.

"Do you feel naughty?" I said with a smile.

The side door opened; Yigal and I hid behind one of the pillars. A group of monks congregated in front of the Buddha altar. Perfectly synchronised, they knelt and started to meditate. The acoustics made their chant hauntingly beautiful. I watched in awe the event that was not meant for foreign eyes. Out of nowhere, an elder of the monks started to chant in a different tone, out of pitch and synch with the others.

Yigal whispered in my ear, "Perhaps he has forgotten the words?"

I burst out laughing, ran out the door, knowing that the jig was up. Unlike poor Yigal, I had already organised an exit strategy in my mind in case it was required. I took a hard right, removed my jacket so I was now in a white T-shirt and casually stood still behind a parked utility truck, pretending to do up my shoelace. Yigal came out of the monastery soon after, running straight ahead with a bunch of monks in pursuit. It was a funny sight to behold.

We met back at the tour bus. I had tears in my eyes from the laughter his actions had brought me.

He too was laughing as he exclaimed, "I was running for my life. It was terrifying. I loved it."

***

Upon our return to the hotel, we decided to have dinner together to recap the day's events. I had most certainly delivered on my promise that the tour would be unforgettable. At the conclusion of the meal, Yigal politely indicated that he didn't want the night to end. I smiled, kissed him on the cheek and left.

***

When the plane touched down at Tullamarine airport, I felt a sense of nostalgia. I had been gone for four weeks and three days. As I headed down the road towards my place, it felt good to be behind the driver's seat of my trusty old Beetle again. I had an associated sense of freedom behind the wheel. It reminded me that I could go anywhere and do anything. I parked my car and walked inside.

Denis was sprawled across the couch, watching TV. "Hey, Talia, welcome back. I started to wonder if you were ever going to return."

"Talia, is that you?" Rhonda's voice called from the kitchen. She came across to me and placed her arms around me. "Thank the stars that you're okay."

I stepped back and smiled. "Why wouldn't I be okay?"

"You left and didn't tell us where you were going or when you were coming back. I was worried about you. I mean, when were you going to tell us you were in Thailand?"

"How did you know I was in Thailand?"

Rhonda diverted her gaze to the ground and Denis sat up to watch the dialogue unfold. I think he was secretly hoping for a bitch-slapping session.

"Rhonda, answer me. It's a simple question."

"Don't get angry at me. I was worried about you. I didn't know what else I could do."

"What did you do?"

"I opened your mail."

"My mail?"

"Yes – a letter came for you in the mail and it was a receipt for payment for flights to and accommodation in Phuket, Thailand."

"So that's how Ethan knew where to reach me."

"Ethan went to Thailand! Nooooo, really?" she said, switching into gossip mode.

"No, Rhonda, he didn't go to Thailand, but he did write to me and posted it to the hotel."

"Ooooo! What did it say?" she said, clapping her hands in the anticipation of receiving some inside knowledge.

"Well, the opening paragraph of the letter, if you must know, said 'NONE of your fucking business'. Geez, Rhonda, do you mind?"

"Sorry, sorry, Talia, it's just that he had been here almost every day for the first week, crying. I guess I got a little caught up in it all. He's such a nice guy and he's so in love with you."

"Leave it, Rhonda," I said as I grabbed my things and headed to my room.

As I stood outside my bedroom doorway, a thought crossed my mind. I called out, "Rhonda."

"Yes," she replied.

"Did you open all my mail or just that one?"

There was silence.

I dropped my bags, feeling a surge of anger as I stormed back into the lounge to look her in the eyes.

"Why didn't you tell us you were rich?" she said, her hands positioned on her hips.

I looked at her body language and was filled with a sense of betrayal. "Are you kidding me? What right do you have opening other people's private mail? You've been busting to snoop and find out more about me ever since I got here. Congratulations. You saw your shot and you took it. Tell me, Rhonda, when do you start choosing to live your life rather than existing through mine?"

She stared at me, tears welling as she tried to think of what to say.

Furious at her inability to speak, I said in a snide tone, "I'm not really expecting an articulate response to quantify your behaviour. I'm going to bed."

As I shut the door to my room, I could hear Denis taunting Rhonda about being told off. Closing the door and leaving their voices behind, I was glad to see my bedroom and to place my head on a familiar pillow. There is something to be said for simple creature comforts. I was exhausted.

***

I woke at midday the next day. Everyone was already at work so I had the place to myself. I had a long indulgent shower, put on some clean clothes and, with dripping hair, went to the kitchen to grab a bite. On the bench there was a note from Rhonda.

Sorry, Talia, Ethan saw your car and knows you're home. He plans to come around tonight to see you. A person by the name of Doug has called several times, leaving no message, and a fellow by the name of Brad called once.

I lost my appetite. Brad had never tried to reach me. The pit of my stomach churned as my mind conjured horrible reasons for him to call. He hadn't left a number, so I called Ruth.

"Hi, Ruth."

"Talia, it's been too long. How are you?"

"I'm fine. I just got back from Thailand. I decided to take a random trip and ended up there for a month. I got back into the country yesterday."

She laughed. "I swear, sometimes I think you and Brad are cut from the same cloth."

"Actually, that was one of the reasons I called. Rhonda said that Brad had called while I was away, but he didn't leave a message. Is he alright?"

"Yes, he's wonderful. He was calling to let you know the good news. I probably should let him tell you."

"No, that's okay. You can tell me and I'll act surprised when we finally get to chat."

"He's engaged to be married. In September, we're going to have our first of four weddings," she sang in a melodic voice.

I chose to ignore her suggestion of four weddings, knowing I had no intention of ever walking down the aisle to exchange vows with another. "Wow, that's great news. I'm surprised Brad is the first to settle. I would have bet it was Tommy for sure." I felt sick inside. I knew I should be happy for him. A part of me was – and the rest of me was contorting into knots. I was officially losing what was never mine to have.

"I know. I thought the same. Wait until you meet her. Suzanna is marvellous. Sammy and her get along and Tommy too."

"Introductions to the family already. He must be serious."

"Talia, when are you coming to visit?"

"I'm not sure, Auntie Ruth. One day soon, okay?"

"Okay, Talia. You know that it's been nearly three years since you left."

"You should let Brad know that you told me. It'll save him trying to call. I'm sure he's busy prepping for the wedding. Pass on my biggest congratulations and let him know that I'm ecstatic for him and his bride-to-be."

"Okay, I will."

"Thanks, Auntie Ruth. Pass on my well wishes to all."

"I will, Talia. Bye."

I hung up the phone and slid to the floor. I could hear the sadness in her voice when she tried to reach out to me. I would feel forever blessed that they offered me a place of sanctity in their own home and with their own family. It was a gift I had received in the absence of my own parents but they could never fill that void. It was not theirs to fill.

I sat there until my legs were numb from loss of circulation. All I wanted to do was climb back in my car and drive as far away from the feeling as possible. The rational part of me knew that this was never going to be the solution, given that I was the constant and would always be present wherever I went. I had to trust that the answers would come.

My first errand for the day was to obtain a Post Office box. I wanted to ensure that no one would ever be tempted to snoop due to my clandestine nature. If they did make attempts, I wanted to ensure that their efforts were not so easily rewarded with answers. I didn't want the money to alter me or the knowledge of its existence to cause people to treat me differently or expect anything different from me. I had no desire to be measured or defined by my wealth.

The second priority was to obtain the rental listings in the surrounding area. I needed space and privacy. I knew that now. I liked to join in the parties and be in among the crowd but I enjoyed leaving them behind just as much. It was time to create myself a home.

I narrowed down the listings to three places. The agent was kind enough to show them to me immediately. I decided on an upper floor studio loft in an art deco building in St Kilda. The view from the large main window overlooked the iconic entrance to Luna Park and some of the bay behind it. I filled in an application and offered a six-month rent payment plus bond. It was accepted on the spot. The keys were to be made available on the Friday so that I could move in over the weekend. I now had the better part of three days to buy some furniture.

The final and most exciting of the errands was to

locate a martial arts trainer. I wanted to continue what had been started in Thailand. I narrowed it down to five studios in the area.

I walked into the first two, spoke to some people and watched a portion of their classes. As I walked to the third one, I wondered if my expectation had been tainted by my introduction in Thailand. The classes seemed sterile and without connection.

When I went into the third studio, I entered semi-disheartened and ready to be disappointed again. The place was empty, with the exception of a man who sat in the centre of the room with his arms folded and eyes closed.

I waited for him to stir.

He didn't move.

I walked towards him, and as I reached the edge of the mat, he spoke the words, "Shoes off," in a direct, commanding voice.

I took off my shoes and placed them beside the row of other shoes that I could now see against the wall.

I walked across and stood in front of him. He chose not to stir. I took a deep breath and sat before him with my legs crossed. I closed my eyes, calmed my breath and cleared my mind.

Time passed and eventually he said, "Good."

I slowly opened my eyes and saw him look into mine.

He smiled, tapped his hands on my legs. "Tomorrow we start training."

He leaped up to a standing stance, bowed his head and walked away.

I rose to my feet, put my shoes on and left to head back to the house. I had found my new martial arts teacher.

Sitting outside the door of my old house was Ethan.

"Hey, you," I said with a gentle smile as I walked towards him.

"Hey, Talia." He stood up and gave me a cuddle. "I really need to talk to you. Please give me this," he said.

"Okay, let's get out of here. If we're going to talk then I want to do it someplace else. Is that okay?" I asked.

"Can I pick the spot?" he said.

"Sure, anywhere but here."

He nodded. As we walked to the car, he kept looking at me.

"What?"

"You're all tanned and looking very fit. It's distracting," he said as he opened his passenger side door for me.

In the car I could feel the exhaustion from jet lag and the emotions of the morning creeping up on me, so I didn't pay any attention to the direction we headed. When we arrived, I look across at him and smiled.

"I come here almost every day just to feel connected to you." His face contorted and tears welled in the corner of his eyes.

"Ethan, I love this place and I love what we did here. I gave myself to you under that pier. I have no regrets about that or the time we spent together."

"Why did it have to end? Why did you leave me?" he asked pleadingly.

"I could see that you were building a future with me that I had no intention of being a part of. The things that you dream about: house, marriage, children, are not my dream."

"So I scared you off with some words?"

"No. They aren't just words. They're your desires. You're in love with me, yes?"

"I am," he said, nodding his head and staring at his hands.

"Ethan, look into my eyes and answer this: Am I in love with you?"

He raised his head to connect with my stare. I watched tear after tear freefall from his eyes. "No," he said in a whisper.

"Ethan, love and be loved. Settle for nothing less."

"Why don't you love me? I would do anything to have you love me."

I looked ahead at the rolling waves, trying to search for an explanation that would be satisfactory for his ears. "I love you, Ethan. Please don't shake your head. Listen to my words. I do love you. I care deeply about you and treasure the time that we shared. I don't want to settle down or get married; these aren't things I desire."

"What then? What does Talia desire?"

"I don't want to be claimed or owned. There is not one part of my being that feels obliged to anyone. I want to harness and live by the rules of free will to continue to do what I want, when I want with no authority greater than myself to answer to."

"Talia, the world is not going to yield before you."

"That's not what I'm asking for. Let's just keep it simple, Ethan. I don't want to be bound to another. I want to be single."

"There's nothing I could do to change your mind?"

"Ethan, don't ever offer to change who you are for anyone. Please, just don't."

"That's okay; I wasn't planning to. I just wanted to see if you would let your guard down to tell me why I wasn't good enough for you. I have girls fall at their feet desperate to have a night with me. I offer you my heart and this is what I get."

"Fuck, Ethan, I don't want to be in a relationship. I don't want to move in together. I don't want to play games like, 'if it's a girl, what would you name it?' I just want to be left alone."

This struck a chord in Ethan. I could feel him seething. He started the car and drove me home without saying another word. As I got out and closed the door, he sped off. I guess he wanted to find closure and to feel some level of hatred for me in order to justify letting me go. In truth, I was now too exhausted to give a shit.

I walked inside the door and could hear Rhonda say, "Hold on a minute, I think she just walked in the door."

I stepped into the lounge where the lizard, Denis, seemed to have a permanent position sprawled across the couch.

As I entered the kitchen, Rhonda handed the phone across to me with a smile. "It's Doug."

I looked at her. "Of course it is." *Fuck me! Is this day ever going to end?*

"Hey, Doug."

"Good to hear your voice, Talia."

"How are things?" I asked.

"Look, I wanted to apologise for the way I acted. I behaved like a bit of a dick."

"I noticed," I said in a slightly playful tone.

"I didn't mean to place so much pressure on you. I know it put a downer on the rest of your trip."

He wanted me to confirm that I was affected by his absence. He was looking for a sign that I had no intention of providing.

"Doug, I've had a really long day. I'm still feeling

jetlagged and I just realised that I haven't eaten a thing, which is why I'm ready to pass out. I'm going to make this quick. I don't want to be in a relationship."

"Not now. Okay, I can wait."

"No, no, no, no, no. Not ever. I am happy being single. We had a great time in Thailand but that's where it ends. I'm not asking you to understand this, but I insist that you respect my wishes."

"I can keep it casual, Talia. I know I was a little over the top in the end, but –"

I interrupted his speech because I really needed this nonsense to stop.

"Doug, I will never in this lifetime sleep with you again. Please respect that."

"Talia, this isn't you. I understand you're tired. Let's organise a time to catch up this week to chat and have dinner."

"No thanks, Doug."

"Well, can we be friends? I'd like to call you from time to time."

"I'm moving out at the end of the week. I won't have a forwarding address or number so no Doug, that won't be possible. Look after yourself. I'm going to hang up now, okay?"

"Really? This is how you –?"

I put the receiver down, turned around to lean on the bench and saw Rhonda standing at the hallway entrance to the kitchen.

"You're leaving us?"

I felt as though I was trapped in some space continuum called 'state the obvious zone'. I wanted to scream: *leave me alone.*

"What did you expect, Rhonda? You clearly have

boundary issues and felt compelled to actively involve yourself in my very private world without invitation. Did you expect me to just accept this shit behaviour?"

"I thought we would talk about it, perhaps you would berate me, but I didn't expect you to leave."

"Rhonda, no more talking. There's nothing to discuss. I'm done. This is your notice, effective from today. I'm aiming to move out this weekend. I'll pay out the four weeks' rent as per our lease agreement. No stress. Thanks to your snooping, you know I'm good for it."

"Talia, I'm sorry. I wasn't thinking. I just got greedy to learn more about you. It was –"

"STOP! Enough! I am done listening to excuses. Just take the consequences of your actions in silence. This is the cause and effect of what you chose to do." I waved my hand to reconfirm my desire to stop talking and walked out of the kitchen straight into my room.

I was starved but could not bear to engage in another conversation. The pulse of yin and yang today were not so equal. I had managed to establish some positive changes and, fingers crossed, closed off a few loose emotional ties.

As I lay on my bed, my final thoughts drifted to Brad. I decided I wouldn't call him back. September would come soon enough. I'd see him on the day of his wedding. This was probably best. Depleted of energy, it was time for me to rest. The next day I was set to start my training and I wanted to become lost in the zone where I leisured in a mental space of nothingness.

***

The next day I rose early, feeling much better. I had a quick shower, grabbed an apple and I was out of there. I had so much to do. I needed to focus on completing the mental list and start my training.

As I reached the entrance to the martial arts studio, I paused for a moment and allowed my single thought to transfer into goose bumps across my body. This was going to be life-changing.

Inside, I took off my shoes and placed them under the BIG sign that instructed people to do so.

How did I miss that yesterday? I thought to myself.

"You were focused on what was before you rather than all that was contained," came a voice from behind.

I smiled. In silence, I nodded and executed a semi-bow.

He inspected me closely with his eyes and then greeted mine when he was done.

"Show me what you know."

Upon my completion of the Tai Chi routine, he walked across to the mats to face me. Initially he didn't move, just stared. I stared back.

Without a word of warning, he stepped into a fighting stance and struck at my head. I instinctively stepped back and, without altering my gaze, blocked his attack. He was incredibly quick and issued one punch after another. I could feel a vibration of power surge as I connected to prevent his attacks.

He stopped and bowed his head without losing eye contact, so I did the same. He stepped back, folding his arms, and burst into laughter. He had an amazing smile. He glowed when he laughed; joy seemed to beam from him.

"You may not know how to fight yet, but you have a warrior's mind."

I was blown away by these words. That was exactly what Boon had said: warrior's mind. What was it they saw in me that gave them that belief?

"I am Master Yen."

I nodded. "I am student Talia."

He laughed again and shook his head. "You're different. I can see that. Here, in this place, student Talia, I will teach you the art of Kung Fu. I will also continue your Tai Chi training and introduce you to an ancient style of Qi Gong."

He paused. "Talia, I will teach. Are you ready to follow?"

I looked him in the eyes and said, "Yes, Master Yen," and I bowed.

"Good, come back tomorrow. We train for three hours six days a week from 10 am. The disclaimer forms that you need to sign, your uniform and the schedule of fees are on the table near the door."

I nodded in acknowledgement and went to retrieve my shoes. As I headed for the table near the door, he said one last thing.

"You must nourish your body. *Eat.*"

I paused at the sound of these words. I let them resonate through me as I reached across, grabbed the paperwork and my uniform then walked out the door.

***

I moved out at the end of the week as planned. I didn't leave a note or any forwarding details. All my mail was now being re-directed to my Post Office box. I registered new contact numbers and made them unlisted so that I was no longer easy to track down. I realised now that the less people knew, the more they wanted. I had no plans to change myself, so I altered my environment as best I could to support my desire to be unknown.

Master Yen and I trained as planned three hours' a day. I spent my afternoons getting a massage and acupuncture to release the tension from the intense training. At home in my loft, I practised some more, read books on martial arts and watched every movie I could find. I was in the zone and had never felt so settled in my life.

Evocation

On occasion, deep in my slumber, I had an amazing recurring dream that would visit my mind's eye from time to time. I didn't know what triggered its visit; I was always grateful when it did.

My parents are sitting at a table, engaged and laughing with one another. I come into the room, leap onto Daddy's lap and get cuddles from both of them. I lie across their laps. Mum strokes my hair; Dad holds my hand and they share stories about their adventures before I was born. In every dream they tell me a different story.

When I was in that space, I never wanted to wake. A moment of time, real or otherwise, was enough for me to feel a connection with them. They were always so happy. They loved each other with a depth that was visible to me even as a child.

In the days after my dream visited, I found a surfacing desire for intimacy with another. I admitted to myself that if I found what I perceived my parents had with one another then maybe, just maybe, it would be possible for me to fall in love. There was a longing in me to have a deeper connection that I silenced. Every time I allowed myself to be with someone he would fall hard against my lack of desire to be with him in the long term. I had decided that until I found my 'other' I would reduce my interpretation of 'happily ever after' to a maximum of three nights. In saying this, most never made it past one.

I found respite in my silence. Men interpreted my lack of engagement as mysterious and it amplified their desire to sleep with me. I could see that I was surrounded by hunger; they seemed starved for lust, love and connection. When I needed sating, I hunted for the man of my choosing and took him to his bed. My own space I reserved because I was committed to entering it with no inhibitions. I showed my hunted how to intertwine our energies, to exchange our sexual passions and left him by daybreak.

I continued my training and for the most part maintained a high level of sexual abstinence. It was less complicated that way. I held true to my values, answered to no one but myself and felt a level of certainty that I was following the right path.

***

"Guys, come. Talia has arrived!" squealed Ruth in a high-pitched voice, racing towards me with her arms wide open. I received her embrace and returned it. I could feel she was crying as I squeezed her tight. She loved me like her own. I felt that.

"Let me look at you," she said, standing back, touching my face. "You look like your mother," she said with a beaming smile.

I nodded. I knew this to be true.

"Talia," called out Shane, who was followed by Tommy and Sam.

They surrounded me, asking a flurry of questions. I looked at them and smiled, giving them all a welcome embrace. It had been so long.

Standing on the porch leaning against the beam, Brad was watching. My eyes were greeted with the same cheeky smile that he seemed to have reserved only for me. I smiled at him as he came over to join us.

"Hey, you. Congratulations. Getting married tomorrow. That's very grown up," I said to him.

"It was the only way I could get you to come out of hiding," he said as he reached across and drew me into his embrace.

While the others laughed, he whispered in my ear, "Fuck, I missed you."

I drew a deep breath to drink in those words, closed my eyes and tightened my embrace. I knew the next couple of days were not going to be easy.

"Where's Suzanna?" I asked. I had not met the bride-to-be.

"She's staying at Bogong riding school lodge with her parents and some of the guests. You know it's bad luck to see the bride the night before."

"The riding school?"

"Yes," he said with that wicked smile.

"Where's the ceremony being held?" I asked quizzically.

Ruth stepped in. "Brad chose the meadow just over the creek. He even marked the exact spot where they're going to stand. Shane has spent the last month building a bridge so the guests can cross the river."

The whole time she was talking I stared into Brad's

eyes and he returned my gaze. He had chosen the place where we had exchanged our first kiss. I didn't know how to process this.

"Come, Talia, I'll show you the spot," suggested Brad as he walked towards the path.

"No, that's okay. I know the place. It's enchanting. It holds special memories for us all. Let's get some champagne to celebrate your last night of unwedded bliss."

Everyone cheered and headed towards the house. I could see that he was disappointed that I hadn't afforded him an opportunity to be alone with me. In truth, I didn't trust myself. When I looked into his eyes, I didn't trust him either. We had to maintain our distance.

***

Brad tried to create several opportunities for us to be alone. I brushed off his attempts, feeling it was kinder to allow him to believe that I didn't care than to leave him in hope that I did. At nightfall when everyone went to sleep, I lay awake in my little bed, staring at the peeling paint on the ceiling. I heard the floorboards creak and a presence at my door. I walked over and opened it. Brad had his head leaning against the door jamb.

He passed a fleeting look at me then focused on the doorknob, saying, "I think I might have had a little too much to drink."

"Brad, you're about to –"

He interrupted with, "Shhhhhh." His eyes were closed as he said, "I need to talk to you. Please, Talia. I need to do this."

I released a calming breath and nodded. He reached

across and took my hand in his. We walked out the door, down the path towards the creek. At the foot of the bridge that Shane had built, Brad looked across at me and then led me into the river. The water was ice cold and refreshing.

There, in the meadow under the witness of only the stars and a partially lit moon, Brad knelt before me. I instinctively dropped to my knees to look into his eyes. He placed both his hands on my face in a gentle embrace.

"Talia, in this life I choose you." Tears streamed down his face. Pushing through his choked voice, he continued, "I need you to know that I have tried. I have never loved another as I have you. I probably never will. Tomorrow I will commit to spending the rest of my life with Suzanna, but you need to know that I chose you."

I nodded my head to acknowledge the words that ate at the core of my being. I knew that I wielded the power to affect the destiny of his next moment. I reached across to embrace his face. I leaned forward and placed my forehead on his, closed my eyes and said the only words I could, "Marry her."

He pulled back his hands and placed them across his own face to hide his feelings as he released the howling sound of his sorrows. I stood and silently walked back down the path out of his sight before falling to my knees and breaking down myself.

That night I dreamt of nothing. I was cloaked in a veil of sadness that had no way of being appeased. I imagined that Brad was feeling the same.

***

In the morning I woke to hear Tommy calling out Brad's name.

I jumped out of bed and ran outside, fearing the worst. "What is it, Tommy?"

"Brad never slept in his bed last night and I can't find him."

"Go check the meadow across the river."

"The meadow? What would he be doing there?"

"He had a few too many last night. Maybe he went for a walk and passed out somewhere. It's just a guess."

Tommy jogged down the path to investigate. When he returned, he had Brad with him.

"Looks like someone didn't want to be late for their own wedding," Tommy said with a laugh.

Brad didn't look at me as they approached. Not a word was spoken as he went past. I felt sick.

***

It was madness trying to get six people ready for a wedding with only one bathroom. I placed my thoughts aside and hopped on the vibe of excitement that Sammy and Ruth were providing. I assisted them in getting ready and then dressed myself. Today the plan was simple. I would quietly stand at the back out of sight and, after the ceremony when people were distracted, I would slip away.

"Talia." I turned to see Ruth standing in my bedroom doorway. "Brad has asked me to make a special request."

My heart sank. "Sure. What is it?"

"He wants you to walk him down the aisle and give him away today."

"What? No. I thought the bride walked down the aisle, not the groom?"

She mustered up a strained laugh. "Yes, that's the

tradition, but you know Brad." She dropped her head to look at her hands as her expression changed to concern. "Talia, this seems really important to him. Please."

"Where is he? I need to speak with him."

"He said you would know where to find him."

I ran barefoot out the door back towards the meadow. He stood before me on the other side of the bridge, hands on his hips, waiting.

"WHY?" I yelled out, breathless and angry.

"If you don't give me away, I'll take it as a sign that you don't want to let me go."

"I have no right to give you away. Brad, this is ridiculous. People are going to be suspicious."

"I don't give a flying fuck what they think. This is about you and me. Talia, I choose YOU," he said, staring down at me. "Agree to give me away today or I won't marry Suzanna."

I glared at him and could see that he meant it. I was enraged by the heightened cruelty of his request. This was his new strategy to evoke a result that was aligned to what he wanted from me. Brad's final trump card.

"As you wish. Be ready at noon. Today, Brad Parker, I *will* give you away." I walked off, knowing that he was watching me.

This wasn't the outcome that he had wanted, but it was the only one that I was willing to offer under the circumstances. This time I wouldn't let my emotions betray what needed to take place.

When I arrived back at the house, I saw Ruth waiting for me. I smiled and placed a hand on her arm. "It's arranged. It will be my honour to do this for Brad."

She released a sigh of relief and cuddled me from behind, whispering, "I don't understand any of this, but thank you."

***

At the stroke of midday, Brad appeared on the porch. I was surprised to see him wearing a traditional tuxedo. He looked across at me waiting for him at the start of the path, gazed down and smiled at the sight of my bare feet. Then he shook his head and laughed.

Standing beside me now, he looked into my eyes, exhaled a large breath and said, "Let's do this."

I placed my arm in his and walked slowly down the path. We paused at the bridge. He looked over for a brief moment at the water and then proceeded to cross the manmade structure. I kept my mind quiet as we were greeted by the stares of a bunch of people I didn't know. I could see that they were curious at the sight of Brad and me walking down the aisle. He held his pace, slow and steadfast.

The space had been transformed by rows of chairs and an archway had been erected and garnished with meadow flowers. A strip of red carpet had been laid to mark the aisle and, indeed, travelling towards where the minister was standing I could now see where the spot had been marked for the exchanging of the vows. When we reached the position facing the minister, I went to look at Brad to say goodbye.

He tightened his grip on my arm and through pursed lips he whispered, "Don't."

I smiled at the minister while I slowly guided my hand across Brad's arm to reach for his hand. Our fingers were now intertwined and he held my hand tight. It was in this moment that I realised that he wasn't trying to be cruel to me. He needed me there.

The music started and people rose to witness the bride walking down the aisle. I gestured for Brad to turn.

This was the first time I had laid eyes on Suzanna. She looked beautiful. I could see that she was confused by my presence and her father was certainly unsure of the situation. I smiled as she reached us and extended my hand for her father to place his daughter's hand in mine. Giving him an encouraging smile, I nodded my head as I looked at her hand. He kissed her on the cheek and placed her hand on mine. I unfolded Brad's arm to place his hand on top of hers. I now had one of my hands below them and one above.

I looked out to the crowd of eyes and spoke the words, "Blessed is this union."

I removed my hands to leave theirs intact and moved to the side near the front row. The minister gestured for the guests to be seated and they commenced the exchanging of their vows. I knew when I saw her look at Brad, beaming with so much love, that he would be just fine. People jumped in the air, clapping to celebrate their first kiss as husband and wife. They walked down the aisle and the crowds followed. He didn't look back.

In the absence of people, I took one more look around before I headed down the path. This time I walked through the creek to allow the waters to wash away all that was unsaid. When I arrived back at the house, I could hear the muffled sounds of celebration. I jumped into my car and drove down the driveway then out onto the open road. I didn't look in the rear vision mirror. I only wanted to see the way forward from here. I felt a combined sense of relief and a surge of unappeased pain. This had been the hardest thing I had ever done.

***

I drove for days, stopping at different country towns. I wasn't in a rush. I had nowhere to be. I just needed to move. Late one evening, I passed through a small country town across the border between Victoria and South Australia. Rows of cars lined a driveway, forty-four-gallon drums roared with fire and some very outdated 60's music was being carried through the air.

I found myself parking the car and walking up the drive. I waved to the first group of people that I saw huddled around a heated drum. I started talking to them and realised that this was an eighteenth birthday party for a guy called Darren. I decided to explore the house.

In the kitchen was a group of guys smoking a bong. I had never tried a bong before. The guy that was just finishing his drag waved his hand for me to join in.

Fuck it, I thought to myself.

I walked across, sat on his lap, took the pipe into my mouth and inhaled the smoke deep into my lungs. I'd had the odd cigarette on a drunken night so this was not the first time I had inhaled. I released the smoke and blew some rings. The other stoners raised their hands in a wave of approval. I stayed there for a while, taking a few more drags before deciding that I needed some air.

As I walked out the front door and onto the porch a lanky strapping young lad blocked my way. "Hello," he said with a delicious smile.

"Hi."

"Have we met? Who are you here with?"

"I came on my own. I know the birthday boy."

"Really? How do you know him?"

I realised that this was more than likely Darren. Still in my cloud of stoned haze, I persisted. "We went to school together."

"And the name of the school is?"

"Glengala, of course. I was there for a year before I had to move, so it was a long time ago." I had seen the name of the school as I passed through the town and felt very clever about my concocted ruse.

His arms were folded and I could see a moment where he was searching his mind to remember.

It amused me so I started to laugh. "You're Darren, aren't you?"

"Yes." He smirked.

I leaped up and placed my arms around him. "I didn't recognise you. You've grown so tall. Happy birthday, buddy."

He placed his arms around me and swung me in a circle, laughing.

"You are really cheeky. Come with me." He took me back into the house and straight into the kitchen.

I put my hands up in the air, yelling, "Boys."

They responded in kind with, "Talia."

I smugly looked across at Darren and said, "They seem to remember me."

He laughed and shook his head. "What am I to do with you?"

***

In the early hours of the morning as the numbers dwindled I felt the warmth of someone at my back. His arms glided across my shoulder and his hands clasped before me.

He leant over and whispered, "Do you have a place to sleep tonight?"

I glided my hands across the expanse of his arms and

unclasped his hands to turn around and face him. "Yes." I nodded.

"So we are agreed then," he said as he reached down, picked me up in his arms and took me inside the house.

He placed me in a room that was lit with loads of candles; the small fireplace crackled with orange embers. The room was sparse of furniture. There was an old wooden chair and the small bed that I now lay in. I looked up at him as he stood above me. He drew a deep breath as if to soak in the moment and then walked out the door, closing it behind him.

Fuck, that was sexy, I thought to myself as I let my mind drift.

I watched the shadows of light dance on the walls. I was almost asleep when the door re-opened. He stood in front of the fireplace, lit a cigarette and watched me. When he was done, he threw his cigarette butt in the fire, extended his arm over his head and took off his top. He had wide shoulders and a torso that rippled with muscles. He watched my eyes inspect his body. As my vision traced down to the edge of his jeans, he unbuttoned them and took them off. I was so completely aroused at his confidence. He may have been eighteen but his masculinity was present in spades. He removed his jocks to reveal his manhood and walked across to the bed to lie beside me.

"Your move, Talia."

I smiled and said wickedly, "Okay. Night, Darren. Sweet dreams."

He shook his head with a smile and pinned my hands down, his face hovering above mine. "You really know how to drive a man crazy."

I said nothing. I bit the bottom part of my lip and stared at him. Releasing one of my hands, I traced the outline of the muscles on his back. He continued to watch me as I ran my fingers across his lips. His erection pressed hard against my body. As I reached down to trace the outline of the exposed portion of his shaft, he groaned. I smiled at this, lifted my head to connect my lips to his. This was the permission he was waiting for.

He kissed me hard, as if to swallow my face whole. I kissed him back with equal intent and could see that this met with his approval. I was like a rag doll in this man's arms. He propped me up as though I was light as a feather; lifting my arms, he removed my top and threw it across the room. He pulled down the right strap of my bra. As my breast was revealed, he took it in his mouth and toyed with my hardened nipple with his tongue. I ran my fingers through his hair and pushed his head into my breast. Reaching down his back. I scratched at his skin. I could feel the welts from where I had been before but I didn't care. He was driving me crazy.

I needed to regain my composure, so I manoeuvred myself off the bed and walked across to the fireplace. Lighting a cigarette, I turned to look at him. He smiled and assumed the same position that I had been in when he walked in the door. I slowly smoked the cigarette until it was no more. Then I reached down and unbuttoned my jeans. He sat up when he realised that I wasn't wearing any underpants. I unclasped my bra, allowed it to drop to the floor and stood for a moment so he could drink in my nakedness.

As I stood before him, he placed his head against my torso and his arms around my waist. Slowly I crouched, using my eyes to guide him to where I planned to be. I had never been in the presence of such a large cock before. It was wide and had sizable length. At first it made me hesitate.

What on earth was I going to be able to do with this monster?

The surface of the head was like silk. I ran my lips across it and gently kissed the edge before running my tongue all the way down the base of his shaft and up again. I wrapped both of my hands around him and placed what I could in my mouth. I played with his balls and continued to massage his shaft as I used my mouth as a portal for his pleasure. His hands remained on either side of his body, his knuckles white from grasping the sheets and mattress tightly. He raised his hips and flung his head back as he became lost in the sensations.

When I knew he was close, I eased myself onto his lap and placed my arms around him. He lifted me up and laid me on my back across the bed and thrust deep inside me. I pushed my legs up in the air and placed my knees beside my ears. He used his arms to brace my legs in that position and jack-hammered his thrusts deep inside. I groaned with pleasure as he pulled in and out over and over. A blinding white intensity of light shudders rose through my body as I had my first internal orgasm. It was insanely delicious. I released a series of groans, wriggling my lower body in delight.

"Come inside me, birthday boy," I whispered.

He arched his back, thrust hard and released himself. The tingle of the vibration of his groan resonated on my neck.

***

The next day Darren walked me around the perimeter of his hundred-acre plot. It had been his grandpa's land and had been passed down to him. At the age of fifteen he had decided to move out to the farmhouse and start farming the land. He leased out a portion of the lot to the local sheep station and worked with them to shear the sheep, which brought in extra money to cover the slow times. He was so focused on what he wanted for someone so young.

As a treat he took me out to dinner at the local Chinese restaurant. The town was small so it was inevitable that he would know everyone in the place. We tried to sit at a table on our own but that idea was quickly thwarted when people joined tables to make one large table. They positioned us opposite one another and proceeded to monopolise my attention.

He mouthed 'sorry'.

I smiled and mouthed back 'you will be'.

Taking off my sandal, I stretched my foot out to rest it in his bony knee. I kept answering the random questions being thrown at me while my toe travelled the length of the inside of his right thigh towards his groin. Just before I reached the sweet spot, his hand cupped my toes and pushed my foot back to rest on his knee. I did it again. This time I was greeted with both his hands clasping my leg around the ankle as he squeezed a warning. I looked across at him staring at me. He smiled, raised an eyebrow and mouthed the word 'don't' then released his grip. I kept my gaze upon him and started again.

He waited until I almost got there before he stood up and said, "Talia, can I speak to you for a minute?"

"Our food's about to come out. Can whatever you have to say wait?" I released a wicked laugh as others joined in to suggest that he sit down.

He walked around the table, stood behind my chair and placed his hands on either side of my shoulders. "No, we won't be long. I promise," he assured them all.

I tapped one of his hands. "Nah, I think I'll just stay here."

Darren bent down. I thought he was going to whisper something in my ear. Instead he picked up the chair and turned it around so I was exposed and facing him. I squealed as he swiftly grabbed my arm, wrapped the other around my torso and threw me across his shoulder.

He slapped my arse and said, "Sorry, folks, she left me no choice. We'll be back in a minute." He walked out the door.

"Where are you taking me? Seriously, Darren, put me down," I said, choking with laughter.

"Oh, no, Talia, you don't get to call the shots today. Not after that little stunt."

In my sweetest possible voice, I said, "Whatever do you mean?"

He roared with laughter at my attempt to sound innocent and placed me down on a picnic table in the park across from the main drag. His body towered over mine; his breaths were deep. "You were driving me crazy in there."

I smiled. "I know."

He unbuttoned the full length of my knitted dress, opening it like a shirt. He looked at me with acknowledging eyes at the discovery that I was again without panties. He dropped his head between my legs and devoured all that I had to offer.

I groaned, "How can you be so fucking good at this?"

He lifted his head to respond, "There's not much to do in the country," and went back to making my head dizzy with pulses of pleasure.

He made me orgasm so hard that I released a series of references to gods and the word 'yes' so loudly I was certain the neighbours would suspect that someone was shamelessly watching porn.

As he stood up, his mouth moist with my juices, he proceeded to button my dress.

"What are you doing?" I said as I grabbed his shirt and reefed him forward.

His hands were on either side of me, his face in front of mine. I could smell me on his exhale.

"I want you inside me," I said pleadingly.

"I know you do, but naughty girls don't always get what they want. You, my dear, are going to have to wait."

With this he stood upright and put out his hands to help me off the table. I scowled at him before accepting his assistance.

Walking back to the restaurant, I buttoned the rest of my dress.

He paused at the door and looked at me. "Do you ever wear underwear?"

I rolled my eyes, shrugged my shoulders and brushed hard up against him as I walked inside.

"Good timing. The food only just arrived," said the waiter.

"Awesome, I have quite an appetite now," he said, patting his tummy.

I let him revel momentarily in the false illusion that the tables had turned in his favour.

We ate the food and joined in the banter. The people seemed nice. Their lives were uncomplicated. The simplicity of their choice to live away from the hustle and bustle was momentarily attractive.

I noticed that Darren kept an eye on me, so I intentionally didn't look at him. It didn't take long for my ploy to work. He started to make references in his conversations to involve me.

"Isn't that right, Talia?"

"What's your view, Talia?"

He was relentless in his pursuit for eye contact and I was determined to deny him.

Then his foot reached across to touch the bottom of my leg. I kept still as he ran his shoe from my ankle slowly up towards my knee. I gently placed my hand out to support his heel. Then I used my other hand to pull off his shoe. I ran a finger across the outline of his sock, removing it too. Repositioning my body on the chair, I slowly lifted my dress and nestled his foot between my legs, his toe resting on my clitoris. I had his attention now.

"Who's up for dessert?" I said, placing my hands on the table. I was now subtly using my lower torso to gently push and release against his rigid toe.

People cheered and reached out for the menus. I placed my menu in front of Darren, who had an intoxicating look of intensity across his brow.

"Is there anything on the menu that interests you now?" I said, continuing to execute gentle movements against his toe. He just maintained his stare.

"Guess not. Me neither." I glanced around the table and announced, "Okay, folks, it was lovely meeting you. Darren and I are going to call it a night."

"Really, what about dessert?" said Marty, the local butcher.

I executed one last thrust against Darren's toe before responding, "No, I'm going to pass."

Rising from the table, I placed enough money to cover our share of the bill and walked towards the exit. Darren followed closely behind, holding the back of my dress scrunched in his hand as he pressed into the small of my back.

Marty called out, "Darren, you've left a sock and shoe behind."

I burst out laughing and walked out the door, saying, "I'll meet you at the car."

***

I was leaning up against his rusted old Holden ute when he came around the corner. I had my arms stretched out, my hands clasped and swinging from side to side.

As he drew closer, I smiled. "That was fun."

He put his large hands on my waist, lifting me onto the bonnet of the car. No words were spoken as he undid his pants. His eyes were staring into mine as he adjusted me into position. My body was perched on the edge of the bonnet so my legs could wrap around his bony hips. The hunger in his loins was evident as he fucked me hard and fast. The intensity of his reaction to the buildup of the evening was such a turn-on. It didn't take him long to climax so I safely concluded that he felt the same. He was breathing heavily as he rested his head on my shoulder.

"I've never met anyone like you, Talia."

***

That night we lay on his bed, with me wrapped in his arms feeling safe, warm, loved. He listened to me speak about Margret and other experiences that I wanted to share. He had his lips pressed onto the top of my forehead and he was breathing into my hair. I knew he was distracted by thoughts about 'us.'

***

The next morning, as I returned from my morning pee, I found him propped up in bed, smiling.

"You have a cheeky look on your face. What are you thinking about?"

"Well, I was just thinking about the other night."

"Yes, go on," I said.

"When you went down on me," he paused, "you didn't swallow."

"Ha! That's what you're thinking about?"

He repositioned himself to lie on his back with his arms behind his head. "Yep, that's what I'm thinking about."

"Are you kidding me? Have you seen the size of that thing? In my defence, I was afraid if I tried I might drown."

With that, I pounced on him, laughing. We had a little play-wrestle before I positioned myself to lie across his body.

Stroking my hair, he sighed. "I have to go to work tomorrow."

"Hmm, guess it had to happen sometime." I knew where this conversation was leading.

"Will you be here when I get home?"

"No, I planned to leave in the morning."

He stopped stroking my hair and wrapped his arms around me, holding me tight against his torso. We lay silent for the longest time and then he said, "I don't want you to go."

I kissed his chest gently and whispered, "I know."

The rest of that day and all into the night we stayed in one another's embrace. The knowledge of the end being near amplified our intensity of connection. Darren engaged my mind and devoured my body with an intense passion to signal that the stakes had changed. He was no longer having sex; he was making love to me.

***

The crowing of the neighbour's rooster signalled the break of dawn. He was a funny character who seemed to feel an obligation to come over to Darren's to wake him each morning. You could hear him running around the outside of the house making a racket to ensure that all heard him. I quietly climbed out of bed to sneak in a shower before Darren stirred. Then I made us a coffee and walked back into the room.

"That fucking rooster. I'm going to catch the bastard and make a soup," Darren whimpered as he stretched and squinted his eyes against the light.

I sat on the edge of the bed and laughed at the idea of him chasing after the rooster.

"Here's a coffee, sleepyhead. I thought farmers got up early?"

"We do, but they also usually get to have some sleep, something that I haven't had very much of since I met you," he said as he put his arm around my waist and shifted me closer to his torso. He curled his body around me and placed his head on my lap.

I stroked his hair and sipped on my coffee. I really hated that I was saying goodbye to him today.

"Talia."

"Yes."

"I have something to say and I want you to listen before you answer. Okay?"

"Sure." I could feel a churn in the pit of my stomach and I closed my eyes.

"I'm in love with you. I knew the first night that we met that I had to have you."

He paused for a moment and I kept true to my word, remaining silent.

"Talia Jacobs, marry me." He lifted his head to look at my face, which now had tears free-falling onto his.

I looked into his eyes and smiled as I continued to stroke his hair.

"I know that you may not know what you want yet, but I believe I have enough certainty and desire to carry us both," he said with pleading eyes.

"Don't cry. I cannot bear to see you cry," he said as he moved off the bed and knelt before me. "Say yes. Marry me."

"Darren, you're amazing. You have been the most unexpected delight. In this space that we created for one another I could feel our love develop and infuse. You and I exist in different worlds. You know that we want very different things. In order to sustain this momentum, compromises would need to be made. You told me you love this place and don't want to live anywhere else. You want to get married and raise a family. If I'm honest with myself, I'm not sure I want to do that. I know how to compromise; I just don't want to. I don't want you to either." I rested my head on top of his head while he remained silent.

I kissed the top of his head, took one last inhale of his essence and said, "Thank you for loving me."

I stood up and left.

Self-awareness

Master Yen was sitting in the centre of the room when I entered for my 10 am training. I sat in front of him as I had on our first day of meeting. I closed my eyes and waited, but I couldn't keep my mind clear. Images of Brad, Darren, Ethan, my parents all flipped in and out on the back of my eyelids like a slide show. My breath became shallow, tears welling at the sides of my eyes. I was so unsettled. When my legs started to jiggle, Master Yen reached across and placed his hand on them. I found that his touch stilled my thoughts momentarily.

"Talia."

I opened my bloodshot eyes to acknowledge Master Yen.

"The raven in you is restless. No point to train."

I stood up, grabbed my shoes and walked towards the exit, knowing that if I couldn't train in this state of mind then I might not be training for a while.

"Talia." I stopped and waited to receive my message. "EAT," was the last word he said before I left.

***

I lay down on the floor in the middle of my apartment and stared blankly at the wall. I was drained of emotion. I closed my eyes and asked the universe to provide me with the answer before drifting off to sleep. In my dreams I saw a fusion of bright colours presented before me. They wrapped around my being like a warm blanket. In this space I felt calm.

I tried to lie still as I heard the sound of a chirping cricket that kept calling to me. I wasn't sure how a cricket could find its way into my apartment but it was present. I went in search of it, knowing that if it stayed here it would surely die. I gravitated to my bookcase, where I was certain it was hiding. The chirps it released vibrated in my ears as I drew closer.

I pulled out some of the books but he evaded me. Reaching across, I grabbed the scrapbook Ruth and Shane had given me on my twenty-first birthday. I smiled as I noticed that the cricket was sitting on the vacant space on the shelf. He was sitting on his hind legs, watching. He leaped out and landed on the book in my hands. He looked at me then down at the book, tapped it with his front leg and jumped off, disappearing in mid-air. I searched to see where he could have landed and then 'Bam!' my body jolted. I took a deep breath and woke. It was a dream.

I was still in a daze; the room was dark except for a beam of moonlight. I stood up and walked to the window to look outside. In the still of the night the moon shone brightly. I smiled as the friendly glow lay upon my face. I went to the shelf and grabbed the book and walked across to the couch. An envelope fell from the pages onto the floor. It was my parents' will. I spent the rest of my waking hours trawling through the pages of the scrapbook and re-read the will.

***

At the start of the next business day, I went about making some arrangements. I packed a bag and organised my ticket. I had decided that I would use the book and the will as a guide for my next phase of discovery. I had spent most of my life observing and not asking questions. It was time to go in search of myself. I wanted to know my parents. I wanted to know 'me' in relation to my parents.

***

I arrived in my birthplace, London, five days later and took a cab to the apartment that my parents had left me. Standing outside the old white building, I soaked in the detail of its façade. I walked up the flights of stairs, arriving at the doorway. I wasn't sure what to expect when I entered. The walls were white and the ceilings high. The hallway was longer than I expected. The first thing I noticed was the abundance of light. It bounced off the white walls and was almost blinding in spots. Dust-laden sheets were spread across the furniture. I placed my bag down and decided to explore.

The main bedroom was big, complete with walk-in robes and en suite. I was surprised to see that there were clothes and shoes there. I ran my fingers through the clothes and could see that moths had been feasting on them. These were my parents' things. The room next door was painted in a pale pink with some motifs of flying birds above a little bed. This must have been my room, I thought to myself as I searched for something that might be familiar. I had no memory of this space.

I headed back down the hall towards the open lounge cum dining room and passed through another door. Smiling, I looked across the kitchen island bench to see the table. This was the space in my recurring dreams. I sat in a chair and placed my hands on the table.

I remember, I whispered.

Maybe all those stories they had told me were ones that they had shared with me here. I was glad to feel some connection with what had once been my home.

***

In the following days I focused on getting the apartment into a functional order. I normally disliked cleaning but this process felt like I was cleansing. It was delightful to have new discoveries unfold as I transferred my energy from room to room. There was an album full of photos of my parents and a few of me, even love letters that they had written to one another. I was starting to solidify an image of my parents.

The contact numbers that Ruth and Shane had provided me in the scrapbook were outdated. I hired a private investigator called Alex to do the legwork to establish accurate leads while I spent my time familiarising myself with London.

Soho was my favourite discovery. Live theatre became a special escape for me. Le Miserables was the first of many shows I would get to see while living there. I easily made friends at the local watering hole. Londoners loved to drink. I became a regular and even took a casual job as a barmaid to experience the lifestyle under the guise of being a backpacker.

There was much joy to be had being surrounded by travellers. They seemed to have a carefree abandon because they were on a sabbatical from whatever their obligations were in their home space. I was focused on piecing together the past but also found myself for the first time thinking about my future.

England seemed like a hop, skip and a jump to everything. I started to take overnight trips to Paris, did tours of the vineyards in Tuscany, spent a weekend in Egypt, sunbaked on the beaches in Belize. My eyes were opened to the delights of exploring different countries, cultures and cuisine. The diverse architecture and its associated history had great allure for me. I bought an SLR camera with a couple of lenses to create visual records of my space and time.

In between trips I caught up with Alex to assess the new information. The first couple of times I went to see him I was disheartened to hear that he had located the death notices of people I wanted to catch up with. *Had I left it too late?* The only active lead he produced was my grandparents on my father's side. They were living in Hungary in one of the properties that I had inherited from my parents. I took the details and decided that I would head across within a couple of days.

***

In Hungary, I had a tour guide–interpreter arranged to show me around. I usually preferred to travel solo but in this instance I felt that I would need to build some rapport with the person who was to assist me in communicating with my grandparents.

His name was Marton; he had a slight build and

a charming smile. Born and raised on the outskirts of Budapest, he started working at a young age in a butchery. Eventually his cousin offered him a job as a tour guide in a travel agency he was managing. Marton spent his nights learning different languages and his days walking the streets of his beloved town, providing the highlights of its history.

Marton took me for a boat trip on the Danube to introduce me to the visual splendour of the river and its surrounds. We had coffee and cake in the famous Alexandra bookstore; a private tour of the parliament, a fantastical neo-gothic structure with the most astounding elevators that I had ever laid eyes on. The time and money spent on creating and now maintaining these buildings to their original ornate standard was hard to comprehend.

One of my favourite parts of the walking tour was looking at the statues. We saw many but none captured my intrigue as much as the *Anonymvs Szobor* (Anonymous Statue) that was located in the city park not far from Vajdahunyad Castle. There was a haunting beauty to the design and a truth to its solitude that resonated with me.

Surprisingly, the nightlife in Budapest was coloured with people of all ages. Most shops offered the Turkish water pipe called a hookah as a complement to the drinks that were being served. On our third night out I decided that we should try one. Marton thought it was hysterical when I explained that the way he pronounced hookah sounded like hooker, which is street slang for prostitute in Australia. This was obviously my first experience using a hookah so there was an endless stream of one-liners that I flipped out to educate dear sweet innocent Marton.

"I've never had a hookah."

"This is my first hookah but it won't be my last."

"This hookah is smokin'."

Our laughter had an effect similar to the one the Pied Piper had on mice. It didn't take long for a crowd to gather at our table to join in the frivolity. The night took an interesting turn when Marton decided to be clever and insisted I try a local favourite drink called Zwuck. It was delivered to the table in a standard shot glass and had a green tinge to the clear liquid. Knowing no better, I smelt it before my attempt to scull. Not expecting such a horrid smell, I pulled a face that made everyone roar with laughter.

I laughed with them, raised the shot in the air and said, "Fuck it!" And I threw that first shot straight down the hatch.

It tasted just as the smell had promised: revolting. It was the worst kind of herbal-infused syrup alcohol that had ever passed my lips. The tradition, or so Marton had me believe, was that you drink the Zwuck and then have a beer chaser. I drank that cold beer and then slammed the glass on the table, which was well received by my now captive audience.

I felt an obligation to return the favour to my band of new friends. I ordered a bottle of Zwuck and a bottle of tequila. I laughed when the Zwuck came out. It was in a little dark-green bottle with a red cross in the centre and Zwuck at the bottom. Initially I had suggested that a skull-and-crossbones was more appropriate as a symbol to warn off the unsuspecting.

As I considered the design further, I concluded that the name Zwuck was appropriate, as you felt as though some-one had Zwucked you across the head when you took a drink. Perhaps the cross represented a suggestion that people who chose to voluntarily drink Zwuck should seek medical help? They all laughed at my banter and watched me line up the shot glasses. One row of Zwuck. One row of tequila.

I had Marton sneak off to the local shop for the rest of the supplies. He returned with a small knife, lemons and salt. I put a small pile of the salt in the centre of the table. They all watched as I cut the lemons into wedges, placing them near the salt. The final piece of the drink mania was in place when the waitress brought over a couple of pitchers of beer and poured a glass for everyone.

I picked up a Zwuck shot, looking at everyone, so they followed suit.

I held it in the air and said, "Give us strength," and sculled.

I then put out my left hand and waved to them so that I had their attention. Sprinkling some salt on my left hand between my finger and thumb, I licked it, threw back a tequila shot and sucked on the lemon wedge. Then I shook my head and squinted my eyes as a reaction to the aftereffect of the very sour lemon.

"Lip, sip, suck," I yelled as I raised my empty shot glass in the air.

"Lip, sip, suck," they responded and did the same.

We all laughed as I took a deep breath, raised my beer and settled in to drinking the cold ale. The rules of the drinking game were 'one in, all in'. If someone took a shot, we all had to. Six double shots and beer chasers later, I found myself watching Marton throwing up on another person's shoes while they were attempting to take a leak in the street. Through my blurred vision I could just see the silhouetted outline of two people kissing and another passed out on the cobblestone floor. I had not been this reckless and smashed in forever.

***

In the morning, I found myself in a foreign bed. The sun lit up the small modest room, revealing faded wallpaper that was peeling in sections. I had no idea where I was or how I had got there. I was thankful when I lifted the sheet to see that I was still fully dressed.

Disaster averted, I thought to myself.

In the background I could hear an annoying buzzing sound. I slowly sat up and propped my head in my hands. I was still partially drunk, dehydrated and dizzy. Nice.

In the next room there was a small lounge with a settee and kitchenette. On the settee, Marton was snoring his head off. He was in a position that looked mighty uncomfortable. I laughed as I tried to wake him and he made grunting noises in protest.

When he had surfaced to a level of consciousness, he smiled and said, "Talia, you are very bad."

I laughed. "I assume this is your place?"

"Yesssss," he hissed as he put his hands over his eyes.

"Thank you for giving me your bed." I received no answer. "Marton, I'm starving. We need to get some breakfast."

"Yesssssss," was all he could say in response.

***

We headed out to find some food. As we walked down the streets, I felt people watching me. When I looked at them they would nod their heads and smile. Some of them even waved and knew my name.

"Marton, why does everyone seem to know me?"

A smirk spread across his face as he shook his head.

"What? Tell me?" I asked insistently.

"You don't remember?" he questioned.

"Hmm, nope," I said as I searched my mind for what I might have done.

"What do you remember?" he said, still smirking.

"Drinking a lot. You throwing up. Me laughing. That's it. I don't remember how I got to your place and I certainly have no idea why all these people think that they know me."

"You have a very beautiful voice, Talia," he said as a teasing hint.

"I sang?"

"Yes. You are also a good dancer."

"What the fuck? I don't remember any of this. Are you pulling my leg, Marton?"

"I don't understand. I am not pulling anything. You sing about love." He continued to laugh.

"Bullshit, I don't believe you. You're making this up." I folded my arms in defiance.

"No. It is true, Talia. You told us about Bred?"

I cringed. I had written poetry and lyrics to songs as a way to release my thoughts. It was my secret artistic interpretation of my emotions about events. Up until now, no-one had known about this. It was something I did for me with no intention of sharing.

"Talia." Marton touched my arm to bring me back from my thoughts.

I looked across at him and half-smiled as I shook my head. "Zwuck."

He laughed. "Yes, Zwuck." He paused and again said, "Talia."

I responded, "Yes, Marton."

He looked sincere as he said, "Your songs are beautiful. You made us cry. He was lucky to have you love him."

I reached out and placed my hand on his shoulder. "Let's get some food. I'm starved." I didn't want to hear any more. I needed sustenance.

***

After we had rehydrated and managed to get some food into our abused stomachs, we headed across to the sector of the country where my grandparents lived. The township was laden with many traditional houses. The cobblestone streets resonated with the echoes of clip-clopping hooves towing carts. This place had managed to retain an olde-world charm that allowed an outsider an insight into what it might have been like to live there a century ago.

Marton took me around the region to show me some of the sites he knew and to visit some that he had heard about but had never been to. That night we retired to our hotel early so that we could recoup. My mind was still abuzz at the idea that I had sung my songs to a bunch of strangers. A part of me wanted to quiz Marton more about this and his reference to my dancing. The wiser side of my thoughts ruled that it would be best to let sleeping dogs lie.

***

Daybreak came quicker than I wanted it to. I was lethargic. There was drool on my pillow, not to mention that my breath was rancid. The Hungarian diet was rich in garlic and paprika. I was thankful that I was vegetarian because the food that I saw served seemed to be saturated in animal fats. Lard was a popular staple here and I could not think of anything worse. I dragged myself out of bed, brushed my teeth and took a long hot shower.

Marton was already at the table, being served breakfast. He acknowledged me with a smile and pushed out the chair, gesturing for me to sit.

"Did you sleep good?" he asked.

"Yes, thanks," I said as I yawned and stretched out my arms.

"You still look tired."

"I feel Zwucked."

We both laughed.

"Are you ready to meet your grandparents?"

"Sure."

"Are you nervous?"

"No, I have nothing to lose."

"I don't understand."

"Well, I never knew them so if I meet them and we don't like each other then nothing has changed. If we do like each other then I have gained two extra people in my life."

"I see," he said, watching me closely. "Talia, family is important."

"I know, Marton. I know." I drank my juice, sipped on an awful cup of over-percolated coffee then left the breakfast table to settle the bill and fetch my things.

***

166

After twenty minutes by car, we arrived at the gates of a property that had a long winding drive. There were aspects of the place that looked like parkland. The established trees were magnificent. Patches of the area seemed to be overgrown by weeds. When we arrived at the manor, I saw the curtain on a front window move. Someone was watching us vacate the car.

I straightened my shirt and took a deep breath as I walked across to Marton.

"Are you ready?" he said with a reassuring smile.

"Sure," I replied and headed towards the front door.

The door opened before I could knock on it. A little old lady stood before us, making an obvious inspection as she glanced up and down at us from head to toe. Marton put on his most charming voice, introduced himself and started to explain who I was. All I saw was a change of expression on her face as her mouth opened to say my name. Her crossed arms were now open and she leaped forward and held me in a tight embrace. I placed my arms around her in kind.

Marton looked at me and smiled. "Talia, this is your grandmother."

I nodded and squeezed her tighter to translate that I now knew who she was. When the embrace was broken she grabbed my hand and took me inside, yelling out to her husband. A lovely little old man came running through the back door. Out of breath, he listened to his wife explaining who I was and then he looked up at me, placing his arms out, gesturing for a cuddle. I smiled and went into his arms. My grandma joined the hug and the three of us stood there for the longest time in a united embrace. I could feel their happiness exude from their bodies.

The better part of the day was spent with them

showing me pictures of my dad as a child, hearing stories about his antics, how he had met my mother, their forbidden love. It was surreal to have this information stream freely from their minds. They took me on a tour of the place. It was truly enormous and very run down. The farm had once been one of the prime producing properties in the district. As my grandparents grew older, they were unable to sustain the workload. People they had employed moved on and things got out of hand.

In the evening after dinner the atmosphere changed. I could see that there was sadness in my grandparents' faces as they studied me. In a low voice, my grandfather asked Marton a question, his eyes staring at the hand his wife was squeezing.

"Talia, he asked if you could tell him how his son died."

I looked across at them both. "Your son drowned. They both did."

As Marton translated, my grandfather placed his hands over his face and wept. Grandma was crying too but she seemed to be focused on consoling her husband. Judging by the look of him, I assumed that it would not be very often that she would witness his emotional release.

"Talia," whispered Marton.

I turned to look at him.

He was crying and shaking his head. "I'm sorry, Talia. I did not know."

I reached out and touched his knee to reassure him. "Nothing to be sorry for, Marton."

I stood up and walked outside to get some air. It had never dawned on me that in my search for answers I would be providing them.

***

Marton and I slept there that night. I had intended to go back into town but they insisted that we stay. I didn't want to offend them so I accepted their hospitality.

In the morning I took Marton for a walk and explained to him that I wanted to help my grandparents to get the house back into a better state and, if they wanted, to look at re-establishing the farm so that it was income-producing again. I felt exhilarated at the thought of being able to contribute to their quality of life.

Over breakfast, Marton told them of my offer and intention to assist them. I was taken aback when they waved their arms and flung back a stream of words. Something had been lost in translation.

Marton looked at me. "They think that you want to fix the place to sell it from underneath them."

I looked at my grandmother and shook my head. Her gaze diverted to the table. My grandfather folded his arms and also would not hold eye contact.

"Marton, please let them know that I have no intention of selling the property, ever. This is their home and it will always be their home. I only wanted to assist them. Everything can stay as it is if that's what makes them happy. No problems."

They both sat in silence for the longest time and out of respect we did the same. My grandma broke the silence by saying something to Grandpa. He looked like he agreed with her statement and then started to reciprocate the banter. Underneath the kitchen table, Marton placed his hand on my leg and gently squeezed. I looked at him staring at them while beaming with happiness. My grandparents were now totally engaged; arms flew around, fingers pointed.

I leaned in to whisper in Marton's ear, "Are they fighting or talking. I can't tell?"

"They are listing all the things that need to be fixed on the property."

I was relieved to hear that they were no longer offended.

***

At the end of my stay we had managed to draw up a list of all the things that needed to be done. I offered Marton a job, which he gladly accepted. He would be in charge of overseeing the repairs, negotiating costs, ensuring that my grandparents received a fair deal. They were so pleased with the idea of Marton assisting. They had all seemed to take a shine to one another.

I headed back to London feeling very happy with the mutual benefits we had all received from our union. It was funny to think that the last eighteen months in Europe could be credited back to a dream I had about a noisy cricket.

At the apartment, I sat curled up on the couch letting the beam of sunlight streaming through the window warm my feet. An image of Ruth kept creeping into my thoughts. I had not spoken to any of them since Brad's wedding. I had written some letters to let them know that I was out and about. I even converted some of the images I had taken into postcards. I did love them; I just didn't know how to be around them.

Ruth continued to be present in my thoughts. It concerned me enough to pick up the phone and call.

"Hello."

"Hi, Sammy. It's Talia."

"Oh, my god, we've been trying to reach you," she said in a strained voice.

"Really, why? Is everything okay? How's Ruth?"

"I'm going to put Mum on. She needs to speak with you."

"Okay." Now I was concerned. I had no idea what the hell was going on but my stomach was churning and I could feel my temperature rising.

"Talia. Oh, Talia, I've been trying to reach you. Where have you been?"

"Hi, Ruth, what's happened?"

"Is Brad with you?"

"No, why would he be with me?"

"You would tell me if he was, wouldn't you, Talia?"

"Yes, of course. Seriously, Ruth, I have no idea what's going on. Can you please tell me?"

She paused for a moment. I could hear her exhalation through the phone. "I received a letter from the IVF clinic that Shane and I used."

"IVF?"

"Yes, just listen, Talia. After I had Tommy, I struggled to fall pregnant. Shane and I tried for a while and then I was told that I had some issues with my fallopian tubes. They had collapsed or something. Anyway, the point is that we wanted more kids and I wasn't falling pregnant. We went through an IVF program and successfully had Brad and then Sam."

"Okay."

"The letter that I received from the IVF clinic indicated that a lab issue had been identified and that I needed to get Brad and Sam tested for DNA verification."

My heart sank. I knew where this was going, but had to pretend I was oblivious to what she was about to say. My mind was swirling and I wanted to throw up.

"Talia, are you still there?"

"Yes, Auntie Ruth. I'm listening."

"The results came back. Sammy is our biological daughter." Ruth was now crying and her breathing was heavy as she continued, "Shane is Brad's father, but I am not his biological mother." She sobbed loudly into the phone.

I raised my hand to my mouth and shook my head. "You are an amazing mother, Ruth. You carried him, you gave birth to him and you love him. Brad is your son. Nothing can change that."

She sobbed for a while and in a meek response said, "I know."

"How did this even get discovered?"

"Apparently, I'm not the only one this happened to. Once they identified that a labelling mix-up had occurred in the lab, a letter was issued to everyone who had attended that clinic."

"How did Brad react to this when you told him?"

"He stood there for a second as I explained what had happened. His only response was to ask whether you knew. When I said that I was trying to reach you to tell you he said he had to go. He left and no one has seen him since. It's been five days."

In my mind I was screaming, *Fuuuuuuuck.*

"Maybe he just needed some time to think? Call Suzanna. She'll know where he is."

"Suzanna is here with us. She was here when I was telling him. We all were."

"Oh."

"Talia, I think he's trying to find you."

"I've been in Hungary for the last couple of weeks so if he came to the apartment he would have been and gone by now. I haven't got any letters in my post box. Are you sure he's coming here?"

"Talia, I saw the look in his eyes. I get it now."

I cringed as I responded, "Get what?"

"He loves you. He has always loved you. Hell, even as kids you were inseparable. You had your own language. His only reaction to the news that I'm not his biological mother was to ask whether you knew. It doesn't take a genius to figure out from there. You're not first cousins; his love is no longer forbidden. Him requesting that you walk down the aisle; all of this makes sense now."

I didn't respond.

"Are you still there?"

"Yes," I said in a small voice.

"Talia, I don't know how you feel about Brad and I'm not asking you to tell me. Given that you left after the ceremony I'm certain I already know the answer. I know that this has been in no small measure hard on you too."

Tears streamed down my face as I anguished at the complexity of this new reality. I so desperately didn't want to feel for Brad. My heart had skipped a beat when she said that we were not related.

"Hello?"

"Yes, sorry. This is just a lot to process. My head is spinning. Go on."

"Suzanna's pregnant. Brad doesn't know. She was going to make the announcement at the family gathering but it never eventuated because my news was delivered first and then Brad left."

Fuck! "Is there anything else I should know?"

"Send him home, Talia. If he comes to you, send him home to his pregnant wife."

"You just need to give Brad a chance to let the dust settle in his mind. I know him. He'll do the right thing."

"I hope that you're right."

I hung up the phone, stood up and paced my lounge, trying to think of what to do. This whole scenario was completely fucked. First he is my cousin, which equals unobtainable, then he is not, which equals obtainable, subject to his divorce. Then his wife is pregnant, which makes him unobtainable. It's in moments like these when I appreciate the overwhelming desire to numb one's senses. The angst, frustration, pain, was surging through my core.

I could no longer stand to be within the confines of the apartment. I put on my sweats, leaped down the stairs, onto the street and I ran like my life depended on it. I went as fast as I could for as long as I could, until the burn in my quads threatened to seize my motion. I felt the symbolism in my desperation to regain my breath. This whole experience was untenable. I walked the streets of London for hours and it was almost dusk when I decided to head home. I couldn't avoid what was happening so I needed to find a way to track down Brad. This was about us and therefore it needed to be resolved jointly. We both deserved a chance to present a voice and agree on an outcome that we both could to embrace.

"Talia," called out a voice from behind me.

I turned and smiled. "Brad." My arms were open as I walked towards him.

He merged into my embrace and breathed in my ear, "I've been looking for you everywhere. Where were you?"

I replied, "Hungary, visiting my grandparents on my father's side."

He pulled back from me and placed his hands on my face. "Wow, really? Talia, that's big. Extending yourself to family."

I laughed and said, "Nice to see I still manage to surprise you."

The expression on his face changed. "There's something I need to tell you. Can we go to your place?"

I pointed to the space behind me. "Sure, it's a block this way."

He sighed. "I know. I've been there every day three times a day for the last week, hoping to find you."

I put my arm in his and walked him back to my place.

Inside, I organised a couple of drinks and we settled on the couch to talk.

"Talia, there's something that I need to tell you."

"I already know," I said as I reached across and sculled my entire glass of wine.

"Ruth called you?"

"I called her, but yes she had been trying to reach me. She was worried about you."

"When did you speak?"

"Today," I said, biting my lower lip and looking at the bottle of wine.

In a surprisingly upbeat tone, he said, "Wow, um okay. I need to know your thoughts."

"Right now, I'm thinking that I should refill this wine glass and scull again." With this, I reached for the bottle.

Brad placed his hand over my glass so I couldn't pour. He glanced into my eyes. "This is important."

I placed the bottle back on the coffee table. "I know it is."

"Talia, in my heart I know that you feel the same

way as I do. I understood why you chose not to express how you felt in the past. That taboo scenario doesn't exist anymore. We're not related."

"You're married," I said in attempt to quash the discussion.

"Talia, I need to know how you feel. I don't want this to remain unspoken. Please talk to me."

I looked into his amazing eyes. "You're killing me."

"Please," he said in a gentle tone as he reached across to hold my hand.

I inhaled and said, "Okay, Mr Parker, I'll do my best to tell you everything from my perspective."

I reached for the wine bottle; Brad snatched it from my grasp. He took my glass, poured the wine and passed it to me with a smile, saying, "Please begin."

"Patience," I said as I took a slow sip. Looking up to the ceiling, I said, "Fuck, where do I start?"

"At the beginning, of course," he said with an excited look on his face.

"Okay, okay, fuck, fuck, fuuuuuck."

"Come on, Talia," he said in a sulky voice, his bottom lip pouting.

I looked at his beautiful face and knew that I wanted to lean across and grab his lip between my teeth and suck on it. He was so sexy; I had forgotten how sexy he was. This whole situation was impossible.

"The night when you kissed me for the first time I honestly wasn't expecting it. There were two key elements to that night that were amazing. One, the idea that you were attracted to me. Two, the surprise at how easily I allowed myself to be immersed in your presence, knowing that what was happening was not ideal." I paused to see what he was going to say.

"I'm listening … for now." A wicked smile landscaped his face.

I smiled back, shaking my head. "The night that you stayed home and we made out in the kitchen, I secretly wanted you to stay with me. I tried to remain composed when you appeared but inside I was doing tummy flips. I wanted to make out with you. My body ached for you. I had every intention of continuing after I took the kettle off the stove. It was only when I turned and saw you there in pain that I realised that I needed to stop. I didn't want to. I would have lost my cherry to my first cousin on the kitchen bench that night. My willpower waned, and there were moments while we were sitting on the floor talking, I wanted to turn and kiss you." I looked across at my hands and sat lost in my own thoughts.

Brad reached across and lifted my face. "Talia, you need to say this stuff out loud so I can hear it too."

"The next morning when you left without saying goodbye, I wanted to die."

"Don't say that, Talia." He put his arms around me and held me tight.

"I know why you did it. It didn't change the fact that it hurt like crazy. I felt that I had been ripped apart. I may have been young when my parents left this world but I cannot recall ever feeling anything like what I felt when I realised you had gone." Tears rolled down my face. Moments of times past were starting to feel present.

"Talia, I am so sorry – please don't cry."

"You want to know so you need to take the good with the bad, Brad. Don't worry about me crying. Let me just get through this, okay?"

He moved in and kissed the tears from my cheek bones with his soft lips and whispered, "Okay."

"You didn't communicate for the longest time. I tried to focus on anything that would keep me busy but you were always swimming in my thoughts. I felt so torn by my desire to be with you, knowing that it wasn't an ideal choice. I was just starting to find my rhythm and BAM! I get your letter. I walked to the river, sat in the water and read it a thousand times. I had no way of being able to appease the yearning that I possessed for you."

I paused for a moment, took a sip of my wine and continued. "I decided that I needed to release you from whatever it was that drew us to one another. I burnt the letter and watched the ashes float free down the river. At the time I felt I had done what I needed to release you. It all seemed right. I guess it would have worked better if I hadn't memorised the letter word for word. I may have burnt the paper you wrote on, but I still carry those words in my heart and mind to this day."

Brad was looking down at his hands. Droplets of water bounced off the couch, making fragments of smaller drops.

"Do you want me to go on?" I asked.

"Yes," he whispered.

"I moved out to establish a life for myself. I think for the most part I was starting to settle in nicely. When I came back for your wedding I wasn't sure if I was going to be able to make it without crossing some inappropriate line. The moment I saw you on the porch, when you whispered in my ear that you missed me, I was in danger of surrendering to my desires. It took all my strength and more to ignore your attempts to spend time alone. When you came to my room that night and took me to the meadow, our meadow, I was blown away by your ability to express how you felt. When you said what you said and waited for my response, I told you what was right to say, not what I wanted to say. I would have done anything in that moment to tell you that I was in love with you. I just couldn't allow both of us to surrender to our desires."

I took a deep breath. "Brad, I have to hand it to you. Your stunt the next day was incredible and once again demonstrated your conviction. I was so angry with you for trying to force my hand. I never wanted to give you away." I burst into tears. I couldn't hold back the well of pain that was surging in me. "That was the hardest thing I have ever had to do," I blubbered.

Brad pulled me towards him so that my head was on his chest and his arms were around me. "I know, Talia. It was fucked. I was just so hurt that I had poured out my heart to you and got back squat. I knew that you felt the same and was hell bent on getting you to admit it."

I continued to cry into his shirt, soaking it with my tears. I couldn't stop myself. Years of frustration and silence had caused a bottleneck in my ability to release these emotions. I wanted to set them free.

"I know," I whispered.

I stayed in his arms for a while, listening to his heartbeat and feeling his warmth on my face as his hands gently caressed my back.

"What else do you want to know?" I asked.

"How do you feel about me now?"

"I love you. I miss us," I said in a dulcet whisper.

"Me too," he said, squeezing his arms around me.

"You need to call Suzanna."

"Yep."

"She loves you deeply. I could see it on your wedding day."

"Talia, don't start talking about Suzanna as a ploy to push me away. I know you feel obliged to be a martyr. I need you not to be this time, okay?"

I didn't reply. I let the silence carry through the room.

In an attempt to emphasise the importance of his request, Brad said, "I want us to share everything that has been unsaid. If I don't do this I'm going to go crazy."

"I get it. I'm just not sure whether this exchange is going to make things more complicated."

Brad ignored my words. "I think I realised I was in love with you from the age of twelve. You were the most extraordinary person in the world. Mum would always remind me to think of you as a sister," he said with a laugh. "Guess that didn't work."

"Yeah, I felt she was always keeping an eye on us. Maybe she suspected that we might cross a line." I lifted my head and winked at him before placing it back on his chest. "That reminds me. I forgot to mention, she told me over the phone that she figured everything out and that she knows that you have been or still do love me. She even used the word 'forbidden'."

"Really?"

"Yep," I said as I nuzzled into the chest hair poking out from his shirt.

"How did you respond to that?"

"I did my usual non-address of the topic and side-barred to another discussion."

"Of course you did. It's the classic Talia misdirect."

We both laughed.

"I don't just love you. I am in love with you. Nothing has changed for me. In this life I still choose you." He placed his lips on the top of my forehead and pressed them to seal his words with a kiss.

I could not escape the reality that Suzanna was at home waiting to hear from her husband, who was in my arms professing his undying love. I also understood Brad's position. He only compromised and squelched his feelings because we thought we were related. This had all changed and now he felt liberated and needed to live within his rights to love me. What a fucking nightmare this was.

"Where are you, Talia? You seem like you're drifting," he said as he stroked my hair.

It never ceased to amaze me how in tune he was to my rhythm.

"I was just wondering about what's next. Do you have a plan?"

He laughed as he released the words, "I want to sleep with you."

I raised my head off his chest to look at him. "Brad, you're married. I won't do that."

He returned my gaze. "I'm not asking for sex. I want to sleep beside you, wake up in the morning with you in my arms. I'd like to experience that."

I shook my head as I sat up. "I don't want to place us in a space of temptation. What if things get out of control?"

In a cocksure tone, he said, "It won't. You have my word. No line will be crossed. Not even if you beg me."

"Hmm, really," I said with a smile. "I tell you what. We can share the same bed with no monkey business on the condition that you call Suzanna and Ruth tomorrow. Deal?"

"Deal," he said with a triumphant smile.

"Don't you smile like you think you have won here, Brad."

"I thought I would have a battle on my hands. You caved quicker than I thought. I think I have won because I was going to call them tomorrow anyway," he said tauntingly.

I placed my cheekiest grin on show. "Ha. Funny. I would have slept with you regardless, because that's the only bed in the house."

I raised my glass and offered 'cheers'.

He took a swig of his drink and sprayed it all over me.

I jumped up, screaming, "Wine stains."

I yelled as I poured the dregs of the wine in the bottle across his face and torso.

He leaped up, pinned me against the wall and rubbed the dripping wine on my face and clothing. There was a moment when we both were panting and staring at each other. He released me and slapped my arse hard as I turned to walk towards the bedroom.

"Ouch, what was that for?" I said, rubbing my bum.

"That's for being so god-damned sexy. You really do drive me insane."

I smiled at him, raised an eyebrow. "You know you could always sleep on the couch if you don't have the willpower to behave."

He smugly replied, "Not a hope in hell. Tonight you sleep in my arms."

Fuck, he is sexy, I thought to myself as I went into the bathroom to shower and change into my pajamas.

***

Upon my return, the lights in the lounge were switched off and a solitary candle flame flickered in my room.

Brad was already undressed and in bed.

"Hey, you," I said as I walked across to my side.

He was lying on his back with his arms folded behind his head. He raised an eyebrow as he looked at my nightwear. "Nice PJs. Are they owls?"

"Indeed they are," I said with a laugh.

"What are you wearing under those sheets?" I enquired, seeing that he was topless.

Challenging me, he said, "Take a look, if you dare."

I swanked my way towards him and lifted the sheets. He remained still as I assessed every inch of his sculpted body. He smiled when I didn't hide the fact that I was using my eyes to drink in his beauty. I was grateful that he was wearing boxers.

"Satisfied?" he said, amused at my lingering gaze.

"I guess you will have to do." I released the sheets and allowed them to float back down onto his divine anatomy.

"You really have become quite sassy, Miss Talia."

I bent over above the flame, looked across and said, "I don't know what you mean." I blew out the candle before hopping into bed.

Brad immediately reached over and pulled me into his arms. "Let's sleep," he whispered.

Easier said than done, I thought to myself.

He inhaled and exhaled deeply over and over until his body relaxed and his mind drifted off to the land of slumber. I, on the other hand, was left awake, enveloped in his presence.

***

"Morning, sleepyhead," he greeted my squinting eyes with an amazing smile.

"Morning," I whispered back.

He kept staring at me, looking so cute lying on his side, his arms folded under his head.

"What are you doing?" I said, watching him watching me.

"I'm looking at you. It's surreal having you beside me finally."

I turned around to face the other way. "You have too much morning energy."

Brad laughed as he shuffled closer to me. The warmth exuding from him made my temperature rise. He slowly slid his hand across to the centre of my abdomen. The expanse of his hand opened to cover my core while he slowly moved his thumb from side to side just under the curve of my breast. I could feel his erection growing rigid as he placed his head into the back of my neck and breathed. Then he started to lightly kiss my shoulder. Electric pulses shot through my system as he pushed his body harder against mine. I took his hand and placed it up between my breasts in front of my mouth, where I kissed his palm.

"You promised," I whispered.

He dropped his head back into the crook of my neck. "I know."

I lay still, listening to his breathing. I knew that if he turned me over I would not choose to have the willpower to stop. After a couple of minutes' silence, he shuffled across and climbed out of bed. I didn't move from my position. I knew that he was standing there looking at me.

"I'm going to take a cold shower." There was sadness in his voice.

While he was gone, I climbed out of bed. I knew nothing good could come of us being in this space. I went to the other bathroom, took a quick shower to freshen up and was waiting for him in the lounge when he came out.

"Let's go out for breakfast. My shout," I said with a smile.

He ran his fingers through his hair while looking around for his socks and shoes. "Sure."

We walked hand-in-hand into the heart of town, straight to my favourite breakfast spot. In retrospect, I should have taken him somewhere else. I was friendly with the staff so I could see their curiosity build. I always had breakfast alone.

"The scrambled eggs are good here. If you're hungry then I suggest that you get the hangover breakfast. That's their signature dish."

Brad intertwined his hand with mine. "That sounds fine."

I placed the order, waved hello to the cook, who came out from the kitchen to acknowledge my presence, and then refocused on Brad.

"Talk to me. You've had the sulks ever since we got up this morning."

He still didn't give me eye contact when he replied, "I know. I'm sorry."

"Brad. Don't shut down on me now. You wanted me to be open and tell you everything. Right now I need you to do the same." He didn't respond so I squeezed his hand. "Please."

He looked up at me with the start of some tears forming at the corner of his eyes. "This is harder than I thought," he whispered.

I reached out and clasped his hands in mine.

"I had this idea in my head that I would come here and get you to tell me the truth. I needed to know that you loved me. I thought that knowing this would help me feel satisfied that I wasn't imagining it."

The waitress came across and set the table. Brad sat quietly, waiting for her to leave. I could see by her body language that she felt uncomfortable with our silence. I smiled to alleviate her concern.

As she left, Brad continued, "Last night, having you curled in my arms was one of the happiest moments of my life." He paused. "I want to be with you, Talia. I don't want to wait anymore. God knows, I've waited long enough." He looked into my eyes.

I was torn inside, knowing that he wanted me to confirm that I felt the same. I just couldn't bring myself to say anything other than, "You need to call Suzanna and Ruth today. You promised."

He pulled his hand out from my embrace. "Don't. Don't do that. I want you to deal with this and not deflect." Running his hands through his hair, he continued. "Stop fucking trying to do the right thing and tell me what you want."

The food came to our table.

"Please enjoy," the waitress said in a sweet tone.

"It looks great, thank you," I replied.

Neither of us touched our food. The world around us seemed to fade as he held steadfast in his silent gaze, waiting for me to speak.

"I've never felt a connection or intensity of love for any man as I have with you. It scares the shit out of me. There's always a reason that causes us to be unattainable. I so desperately want to shut down how I feel, but you keep demanding me to be present in my emotions. I want to fantasise about the idea of us, I do. I just know that life seems to pull us apart. You may be the man of my dreams that accidentally manifested in the wrong form. Forever to be my eternal unrequited."

He leaned in and took up both my hands again. "No, Talia, that's just it. I am not unobtainable anymore. Don't you see? We're not related. There's nothing stopping us now. We can be together."

I felt trapped. I wanted to tell him that his wife was pregnant but knew that it wasn't my place. That was hers to share with him. I was also conscious that I ran the risk of him interpreting my delivery of this news as a deflection. I couldn't allow that. This was hard enough as it was.

"Let's get out of here; I've lost my appetite," I said as I stood up.

The waitress came to the table. "Was there something wrong with the food?" she enquired.

"No, it was perfect." I smiled as I placed the money on the table to cover the bill.

We both walked out the door in silence. All this talking and I still felt restrained by my knowledge and desire to do the right thing. There was a sensitive balance that had to take place. I knew he didn't want me to be the martyr. Fuck, I didn't want that role either. If I let go of all I knew I would have reached out and kissed him passionately and told him that I wanted him to be with me too.

We gravitated towards a bench seat in Hyde Park. As we sat down, he said in a low voice, "I need you to fight for us. I know that you're worried about Suzanna. I've thought about her too. I love her. I was just never able to fall in love with her."

I shook my head. "That makes no sense. Why did you marry her?"

He took a deep breath. "I've been with a lot of women. She happened to be the one that I cared about the most out of all of them. I resigned myself to the fact that you and I were never to be, so I decided that I would make a life with her."

"Are you happy together?"

Initially he didn't respond.

I waited.

"It's not that simple. Yes, we are happy but it's happiness in the absence of my unfulfilled desire for you. I was as happy as I could be."

I leaned forward and placed my head in my hands. Brad stroked my hair as I rocked gently backed and forth. I was trying to process everything. If I let go and allowed myself to stake a claim on him, was I deciding the fate of their relationship? Could I conclude from what he was saying that perhaps I was doing her a favour because this freed her to find someone who would return her love? This was so fucking hard.

He leant in and placed his lips on my neck. "Talia, talk to me," he whispered.

I shook my head as I lifted myself upright. "You're right," I said, shrugging my shoulders.

"I am?" he responded with surprise.

"I do default to playing the role of the martyr. I self-sacrifice, especially when it comes to you."

"And …?" he said, encouraging me to continue.

"You win." I knelt before him and took his hand as I watched his face light up. "I am madly in love with you. I want to be with you too. It took all my energy not to respond to your advances this morning."

He leaned down to kiss me as I turned my face away. "I can't. Not like this. You need to do the right thing by Suzanna and I don't want to sleep with a married man."

As I stood up, he said, "I'm sorry. I got swept away for a moment."

I half-smiled. "It's okay. Let's head back to my place. There's something I need to show you." I offered him my hand.

***

In the apartment, I directed him to the lounge. He sat on the couch with his hands on his lap, waiting. I retrieved a worn old shoebox from my wardrobe and placed it on the coffee table in front of him.

"What's this?" he asked with an eyebrow raised.

I knelt down on the other side of the table and opened the lid to reveal a mish-mash of items.

"This box contains a little girl's secret desires. Poems, songs, undelivered Valentine's cards; there's even a mixed tape. It's all about my unrequited love for you."

He placed his hand on the lid of the box. "Talia, I don't know what to say."

I rose and walked across to stand near him. "There's nothing to say. You asked me to tell you the truth. I guess this box shows you my truth. I'm giving it to you. I hope it provides you with the confirmation that I denied you all these years." I bent down and kissed the top of his head. "I'm going to leave you the keys to my place. I need some space to gather my thoughts and give you some time to catch up on a lifetime of unspoken words." I started to walk towards the door. "It will be early morning in Australia from about 10 pm our time. Suzanna is still at your mum's so it's best to call her there."

Brad looked puzzled at the news that she was still at his parents' place. "Okay," he said.

I partially opened the door. "Brad, no matter what happens tonight, if after talking to her you change your mind, I will accept whatever you choose to do. I'm going to trust that the decision you make will be the right one for both of us. Okay?"

He laughed. "Talia, there's nothing that anyone can say or do to stop me from being with you. We're finally going to be together. That's all that matters to me now," he said in a reassuring tone.

I closed the door behind me and whispered the words, "I love you."

***

I spent the remainder of my day in the Museum of Modern Art. I needed to get lost in a visceral distraction that didn't involve any emotional contribution. I had to trust that in the presence of our exchanged truth the path would be self-determined. I would respect his decision to stay or go and would adjust accordingly.

I had no intention of going home until Brad had spoken to Suzanna. He would need some time to think about everything when he understood his reality. I was sick of roaming around aimlessly, so I booked a room in a boutique hotel, ordered room service and took a hot bath. I set the alarm for 11 pm and wrapped myself in the duvet. Instantly my body surrendered to the comfort of the bed and I thankfully fell asleep.

***

The sound of the alarm woke me. It felt as though only moments had passed. The clock was flashing 11:10 pm. I put my shoes on, grabbed my things and headed home. I didn't want to pre-empt what was going to happen but already knew inside how this was going to pan out. The door was unlocked and all the lights were off. I walked inside and could see Brad's silhouette against the backdrop of the window.

"Brad," I said as I stood in front of him.

His arms were wrapped tightly around himself like he was trapped in an invisible straitjacket. Pain surged to the surface as his face contorted. Snot splattered out of his runny nose when he blurted, "She's pregnant."

He bent his head down and placed it on my shoulder and howled.

I put my arms around him and burst into a manic suite of tears. "I know," I said in between sobs.

Eventually I managed to pry his arms apart. I placed him on the couch and lay between his legs across his chest. We didn't speak a word. There was no need. I knew Brad and Brad knew me. I just listened to the beating of his heart, lost in the rise and fall of his breathing until I drifted off to sleep.

"Talia, are you awake?"

I opened my eyes and shifted my position so that my hand could get some circulation going again. Pins and needles surged up my arm as I clenched and released my fist.

"Morning," I said in a husky voice.

"I'm going to have to organise my flight home," he said in a sombre tone.

"It's okay. I already reserved you a ticket. It leaves at 6 pm tonight. We need to be at Heathrow by 4 pm to check in your bags."

Brad readjusted so he was sitting up. Folding his arms, he asked, "How did you know I would leave?"

I rubbed my swollen red eyes as I sat up too. "Truthfully, I didn't."

Annoyed, he persisted, "Then why would you book a flight for me, Talia?"

I took a deep breath, placed my palm across his chest. "Because, Brad, you're the type of guy that wouldn't leave his pregnant wife."

He put his hand on top of mine and pressed it hard into his chest. "The fact that you're going back to meet your commitment makes me love you even more," I said, tears once again surfacing.

He reached across and pulled me into his arms. "I'm so sorry, Talia. This is so fucked up."

I shook my head. "Don't say that. You're going to be a dad. That's golden, Brad. I don't know Suzanna, but I know you. If you married her then she must be pretty awesome. It's going to be amazing. I promise."

I looked across the lounge room floor. Brad had spread the contents of the shoebox on the carpet. I blushed at the thought of him knowing everything. I was completely exposed.

"It's okay, Talia. Your secret's safe with me," he said in a satisfied tone.

I buried my head in his chest and shook my head.

He let out a little laugh. "You had a major crush on me from the get-go."

I pinched him. "Stop it."

He squirmed out of my pincer grip and then changed his tone. "I'm sorry for all the pain I caused you."

I squeezed my arms tight around him. "No regrets, Brad. This was good for both of us."

He shook his head in disagreement. "Good how?"

"I had convinced myself that my heart was like rubber. People would try to penetrate but the harder they tried the further they would bounce. The last couple of days have showed me something that I didn't allow myself to acknowledge. In your presence, my heart was more akin to a sponge. It absorbed everything you were willing to offer and when squeezed it would release in kind. It showed me that it's possible."

He stroked my hair. "What's possible, Talia?"

"For me to fall in love," I said in a soft voice.

He exhaled at these words and pressed himself hard against my body. The rest of the morning was savoured in silence.

***

Heathrow airport was busy as usual. Brad and I were lost in an ocean of people impatiently swarming the queues. We weren't going to have any more private time so this was it.

"I hate this part," I said, breaking the silence.

"Me too. It always seems like we have to do this," he said, pouting his delicious lip.

"Yep." I smiled.

"Talia, I'm going to be selfish and ask you to do something for me."

I looked at him.

"Don't exclude me from your life. We've wasted so much time already. I want a find a way that we can provide a space for one another."

In a small voice I confirmed, "I'd like that." I knew that he was putting on a brave face.

"I'll send you a text when I arrive home. It would be nice if you sent a reply to my messages from time to time."

I laughed and nodded my head. I didn't want to cry

but I knew if I stayed any longer I might. I reached over and placed my arms around him. I squeezed him tightly and then released him.

"I'll see you, Brad." I turned to walk away.

He grabbed my arm, swung me around and put me back in his embrace. "I'm never ever going to forget the time we spent, Talia. Fuck, I love you so much and to know that you love me is priceless. This is what will carry me through. I love you. Never forget that I will always love you," he sobbed and I burst into tears.

I held him and didn't care that people were now circling around us to maintain the flow of the queue. I wanted to die. Once again I was to give up the only person that I loved. I moved my head to face his and I kissed him passionately. Tears rolled into our mouths as we exchanged our intensity for one another. I eventually pulled back, took one last look into his moist, swollen eyes and walked away.

Free Will

Weeks had passed since Brad had left. Suzanna had embraced him with open arms and all was as it should be. I, on the other hand, struggled to stay in the apartment. I could see us on the couch, in the bed. I needed a distraction so Paris became my escape. I made a few friends there and felt comfortable lost in the spaces between routine. Most of the people I hung out with were nocturnal creatures, which suited my own biorhythm. It was all happening at a time when vampire movies and gothic dress was becoming an acceptable social norm.

Lena was an accomplished artist who held a studio near the famous Moulin Rouge. Her boyfriend Enzo was fifteen years younger than she was. At first glance he appeared masculine, self-confident, until she stepped in the room. Once Lena was present he became a subservient child who waited on her shamelessly.

I spent a lot of time in her studio. Initially I went in there to do a photo study of artists in Paris to develop my photographic portfolio. For my short course in photography, I had an assignment to create a portrait study based on a theme. The lecturer Jean Paul had suggested I explore artists. When I agreed, he introduced me to Lena.

One day as I was entering the studio, a super-hot bloke was walking out looking a little dishevelled. I could see that Lena was putting her stockings on and pulling down her skirt. She didn't seem to flinch at my presence.

"Come, Talia." She gestured with her long arms.

"Lena, did you just have sex with that man?" I said, partially laughing.

"No, not sex. He just gave me pleasure. You know …" She waved towards her nether regions.

"Did you and Enzo break up?"

She laughed at the idea. "No, Talia, this is nothing. Enzo knows I am seeking pleasure with many men." She reached for a smoke and offered me one.

I took a cigarette, lit it and paused to think about this.

"Dis is normal, Talia. A woman must take pleasure, no?" she said, waiting for my response.

"I guess where I come from they think a little different. You know: one man, one woman."

She laughed loudly. "Dis is not possible. To do dis and be happy, not possible."

I smiled; given my track record I wasn't going to place a negative measure on her way of thinking. It was actually refreshing to see a person executing a lifestyle that deviated from the mainstream. I was in a phase where I appreciated different, and life in the presence of Lena was most certainly that.

It didn't take me long to decide to move across to Paris for a while. I was starting to explore aspects of my creativity through photography and Lena took it upon herself to teach me the basic principles of drawing, painting and sculpting. She allowed me to use a space at the back of her studio that I converted into a darkroom.

Jean Paul and I maintained contact after I had completed my short course. He would join me in the darkroom and teach me different techniques. I discovered that developing images in and of itself was an art. A simple variance in exposure time could transform an otherwise ordinary negative into a visual marvel. I was completely immersed in black-and-white photography. I found that I could evoke mood and depth easily in this monochrome spectrum. The fusion of white to grey to black provided an endless playing space that stretched the boundaries of what I chose to see within any given image.

One evening while out with the crew, I explained to Lena that I wanted to try my hand at photojournalism. It wasn't to sell, rather to practise the art of telling a story without the use of words. Jean Paul had taken me to see some exhibitions of photographers who specialised in this field and had introduced me to people who were actively making a career from their cameras. The world was different to me when observed through the eye of a lens.

"If you want something to photograph, I will show you tomorrow what you must do," said Lena, gesturing to Enzo to rub her feet.

"What do you have in mind?" I asked, while staring at Enzo, who was now on the floor kneeling before her.

"Trust, Talia, tis good for you to see," she said, trying to get my attention.

I couldn't help myself. "Why is Enzo sitting on the floor rubbing your feet?"

I had always watched the way she treated him and more importantly the way he allowed her to treat him and felt that it was demeaning. Now we were sitting at a table in a crowded hip club with six others. And still, one gesture of her hand and he did her bidding.

Lena swung her head back and laughed at my question.

Jean Paul leaned in and whispered, "It's okay. This is what Enzo likes."

I looked at Jean Paul and nodded, more to acknowledge his words than to suggest that I even remotely understood. I could not imagine being subservient to anyone. To look at Enzo – the guy had a massive build and was attractive, and in the absence of Lena he appeared to be self-assured. The dynamic between them was beyond me.

Lena raised her glass. "Tomorrow, Talia," she laughed, "tomorrow."

All the others at the table laughed with her. They shared some inner-circle joke. I just smiled, shook my head and lit a cigarette.

Lifting my glass of red in the air, I said, "Tomorrow."

***

The next afternoon I met Lena at the studio.

"Do you have your camera?" she said, looking at my hands.

"Of course." I patted my camera bag.

"Come," she said as she disappeared behind a curtain and through a side door.

The room we entered had stark white-tiled walls. The overhead lights were small but provided a good amount of light as it bounced off all the white.

Lena stood at the entrance of a doorway and said, "Never take pictures of the faces."

I still had no idea what I was supposed to photograph but assumed now that it involved people. "Okay," I responded.

We went through another doorway that proved to be the entrance to a hallway that had a network of rooms branching off on both sides. Each room was painted a different colour and contained different furnishings.

The thought crossed my mind that perhaps Lena was a 'Madam' and these were the different rooms she used to have sex with her clients. It made sense. All these men constantly came to her studio and she didn't hide the fact that they were engaged in coitus.

I stopped halfway down the hall.

What if she wants me to take images of her fucking these men? Is that why she said no faces? Why would she want me to take photos of that? It made no sense.

"Lena, what do you want me to photograph?"

She swung around and said in a commanding voice, "I am Mistress le Vour."

What the fuck! She's gone flippy narna. Mistress le Vour, seriously?

I composed myself. "Okay, Mistress le Vour, what do you want me to photograph?"

She snapped, "SILENCE."

My temperature rose. It pissed me off that she had raised her voice. I was just about to turn and walk out when I heard someone crying. It almost sounded like a baby in the distance. I could see a smile creep across Lena's face as she turned and continued down the hallway towards the entrance of another room.

Against my better judgment, I followed Lena. The room was as stark as the first room we had entered. There was only a couch and a wooden chair.

"Sit." She gestured at the couch.

I sat and tried to identify where the crying was coming from.

"Talia, you must not have judgement here."

I shrugged. "Sure. I have no idea what's going on, but sure."

Her demeanour changed back to the Lena I knew. She smiled. "Wait here." And disappeared into a side room.

I was fixated on the sound of someone crying. It was hard to tell where it came from, as it seemed to wane off into the distance and then start again. When Lena reappeared she had changed into a costume that entailed plenty of leather belts and straps revealing a lot of skin. She had a rocking body for a woman of her age. She held a crop in one hand and a length of strap in the other. The mask that she wore across her face was made up of straps. I wondered if it was designed intentionally to emphasise her mouth. The blood-red lipstick was placed perfectly across her pouty lips. She stood there to allow me a moment to appraise her. The boots she wore went all the way up to her mid-thigh. How she stood in those heels let alone walk was nothing short of impressive.

"You like?" she asked, standing tall with her hands of her hips.

"You look amazing." I was genuine in my response. She did look amazing.

"Good," she said as she walked with a swank into the centre of the room.

When she turned to face me she yanked on the strap and out from the shadows of the doorway a man came stumbling forward. "This is my gimp," she said in a matter-of-fact tone.

The man was dressed from head to toe in a super-tight leather outfit complete with a mask that had a zipper where his mouth should be and only two cut-outs for his eyes and breathing holes for his nose.

Lena smiled and I knew my expression must confirm that I got it now.

She was some kind of sadomasochism bondage mistress or dominatrix. In retrospect, it made sense.

Lena seemed pleased that I didn't react to the introduction of her gimp. She yanked hard at the leash that was attached to a thick, studded collar on his neck.

"On all fours, you dog," she cussed.

He didn't hesitate to obey her command.

She gestured to me to walk across to him.

I stood beside him.

"Sit. He will bring you."

I half-laughed at the suggestion. "No, that's okay. I'm happy to walk." I wasn't going to sit on his back. It was bad enough she was going to make him walk on all fours across hard tiles. The poor bastard didn't need me as a dead weight.

"Talia, if you do not sit, I will beat him."

I looked at Lena and saw by the expression on her face that she meant it. I didn't understand her relationship with the gimp but I did know that I didn't want him beaten because of me. So I sat on the back of the gimp and let him follow Lena down the hall.

Yep, today was going to be just another ordinary day, I thought to myself as I muffled my laughter.

Lena opened a door and walked straight in. As the gimp carried me closer, I could hear a music box playing. The room was decorated in wallpaper that had unicorns jumping over rainbows. I didn't feel too good about the idea of a child being raised in this environment. Consenting adults doing weird shit to each other was fine but kids? Hmm, no. That didn't sit right with me.

"Come and look at my baby," she said, beaming with pride.

I cringed at the confirmation that there was a child in that cot. I tapped the gimp's shoulder to let him know that I was about to hop off and walked across to stand beside Lena. I looked in and then looked at Lena. She smiled and encouraged me to look again.

Fuck me dead! It was a full-grown male, naked except for the enormous nappy wrapped around his distended, hairy belly. He appeared to be sleeping and was sucking his thumb. I was mesmerised. Looking at this made me feel that riding a gimp was normal.

"Come," gestured Lena.

I turned to follow her. She stopped, looked at me and then at the gimp. I smiled and shook my head as I mounted the gimp again. She walked out the door and my trusty steed followed. What could she possibly want to show me next?

We entered a room that was covered wall-to-wall in all types of implements. I had seen some items before: spank paddles, dildos, butt plugs, pearls, nipple clamps. I was no prude but some of this stuff looked nasty.

"I assume this is your tool room. Impressive. It's almost as diverse as my collection," I said with a laugh.

Ignoring my attempt to throw in some humour, she said in a commanding voice, "This is where they get to pick naughty or nice."

I could see by the array of whips, chains, handcuffs and gags that naughty involved pain. Lots and lots of pain.

The final room she took me into had a naked man strapped to a chair. He was blind-folded, had a gag in his mouth and his arms were secured above his head by chains. A length of metal bar was attached to either side by tight chains, forcing his legs apart. I could see that there was something hanging off his balls. I cringed when I realised those purple grapes of his were weighted down.

Lena walked to the man and without saying a word pulled at the chains attached to clamps on his nipples. He was initially startled at her touch but released an elongated groan when she yanked and twisted. I realised that he had earplugs in too, removing some of his key primary senses of sight and sound. He was forced to be present to the pain. As Lena stepped back, a small stream of blood trickled down his chest. She gazed upon him and smiled with satisfaction.

We went back to the room with the couch, where I alighted from my chariot and stood in silence looking at Lena.

She waved her hands in the air. "We make exhibition of your work." Then she walked out of the room with her gimp at her side, not giving me an opportunity to respond.

I decided to leave to allow myself some time to absorb what had just happened. I wasn't freaked out. I know most people would have been. I felt overwhelmed, trying to process what I had witnessed while also being very conscious that I was in a privileged position to be introduced to a world that most would ridicule.

I headed out to my favourite coffee house, positioning myself in the outside section. As I placed my order for a coffee and lit a cigarette, I watched people walk by. My shallow insight into the house of Mistress le

Vour made me pay more attention to people in general. I allowed myself to get lost in my thoughts as I listened to a man on the street play his saxophone.

What makes a grown man want to wear a nappy and suck his thumb? I could appreciate the symbolism of a baby having no responsibility, relinquishing all independence to become dependent for nourishment, shelter, protection and love. It was just such a large leap from the idea of regressing to that headspace versus acting it out. I was going to have to accept their choices in order to do the photo-study justice. I lent myself to the idea of developing more of an abstract imagery, playing with the extremes of light and shade. It would be challenging not to include their faces and to try to tell a story that didn't objectify them.

"Talia." I looked up to see Jean Paul coming across to my table.

We executed the obligatory air kisses on each cheek. "Hello, Jean Paul, please have a seat."

"Have you started taking your photos yet?" he said with a curiosity that made me guess he knew more than I had previously realised.

"No, not yet," I said, reaching for a cigarette.

Jean Paul leaned forward to provide the light. "Is there something wrong?"

I observed the expression of concern on his face. "No, I just wanted to take some time to plan how I was to do this. Lena is suggesting an exhibition of the work. I feel an obligation to ensure that it's captured in the right way. The irony is that I have no idea what is the right way. I'm uncertain of what I'm seeing because I can't relate."

He sat back, smoking his cigarette, and smiled.

"Do you know what Lena wanted me to photograph?" I asked.

"Yes." His response was shorter than I wanted it to be.

"Have you ever taken photos for her in that space?"

He took a long drag of his cigarette before answering. "No." The half-smile on his face made me feel he knew a secret I didn't.

"Jean Paul, what is there that you're not telling me?"

He patted my hand. "I am just happy that you are thinking about taking the photos."

"Is there a reason Lena didn't ask you to take the photos? I'm an amateur and you've been working and teaching the art for years. It doesn't make sense."

Exhaling the last of his cigarette smoke, he rose to his feet and said, "Talia, you are better than you think." He smiled and waved before walking off.

I sat there observing the passing world for the rest of the afternoon and a portion of the evening before I headed back to my loft to get a good night's sleep.

Once inside, I noticed that my mobile was beeping. I had a message.

It was Brad giving me an update on how things were going. He seemed settled in his life now. I didn't tend to text him first; I only responded when he reached out. I was glad that he was trying to create a space where contact could be maintained. I just didn't feel obliged to be the one to make the first move. He carried all the risk and had something to lose so I allowed him to guide me on his contact requirements. I knew that Brad would have wanted me to be more available. I just wasn't convinced that it was the right thing to do. In the absence of me, he could allow himself to fall in love with Suzanna. I wanted that to happen for him, for them.

I sipped a glass of wine while reading his textual essay. It was surreal to think that one moment we were in each other's arms and the next I was being introduced to the world of fetishism and bondage. If there was one thing I was learning about my life – it was unpredictable.

I replied to Brad, letting him know that I was fine. I told him about the art lessons and my exploration of photography and how much I loved Paris. I didn't mention anything about riding a gimp or observing a grown man in nappies. This all still seemed too fantastical to me, let alone discussing it with people. I thought this chapter of my life would be a closed one. There was nothing to be ashamed of, but it was easier not to have to explain. I snuggled under the sheets and went to sleep. Tomorrow I would do some research.

***

In the light of a new day I decided that I would spend some time gathering information about the world to which I had been introduced. I eyeballed sex shop sites to see the diverse implements that were on offer and read Wikipedia definitions of concepts such as forniphilia. I had no idea that there were so many people in this world who were into such a diverse range of stimuli.

I was a little confused during my research, as I kept getting spam invitations to a Teddy Bear convention. It was only after I resigned myself to click on the link that I was taken to a site created for people who were ursusagalmatophilias. I couldn't pronounce it but understood from the pictures that people were obviously turned on by being intimate with teddy bears.

I spent the entire day scanning page after page of information. I read the terms and conditions for submissives and dominants. I learnt about the concept of safe words and the repeated warning against setting no limits. Soft and hard limits were encouraged. This realm was filled with rules and the illusion of submission and control. All of these concepts were driven by suggested free will.

A dominant had to abide by the parameters that the submissive set. Did that not default to the submissive being in control and the dominant being the slave? None of this made sense to me. I felt I was a dominant character, strong-willed, independent, yet I possessed no desire to dominate anyone. I imagined that I would find the obligation cumbersome. It was a big responsibility to reign over a submissive. I couldn't imagine the attraction in having someone surrendering his or her conditional will to me.

The deeper I fell into my research, the less I could relate to the choices these people made. There were a couple of things that were evident to me. One was that the world outside of their common brethren judged them harshly. The second was the amount of sites, information and detail available indicated that this may not be a practice of the minority.

I was living in a day and age where globally people were still being ostracised for choosing to live in same-sex relationships. Marriage and adoption of children was not a legal option and in some places the punishment was known to be public raping or stoning for homosexuality.

I had never been sexually attracted to women. Regardless of that, I would still like to think that if I happened to cross paths with someone I wanted to be with, the world would not sit in judgement. What business was it of theirs anyway?

Resurfacing from the inter-porn super-highway, I appreciated the evident readjustment to my perspective. Threesomes, swingers clubs, all seemed so vanilla now.

I decided to accept that I was not going to relate to their space, but I intended to respect it. They were not going to be a spectacle, at least not the way I depicted them. I wanted to go in there and capture the essence of their beauty, honesty and desires. The rest would be left to the observer to interpret how they chose.

***

It took me the better part of two months to capture a series of ten images of each of ten subjects. Every night I entered the space, not resurfacing until morning. I took thousands of images from hundreds of angles. I played with studio lighting and different backdrops until I was satisfied with the outcome. Lena and I had an agreement that nothing would be discussed or shared. I didn't want my creative thoughts tainted. If I was to play in this space then I wanted to do so without influence.

"The gimp, he likes you," she said as she walked into the tool room.

I was in the process of setting up a mini studio to take individual images of the implements.

I maintained focus on the task at hand as I asked, "How do you know? He never speaks."

She scoffed. "He told me dis yesterday when we were out to lunch."

I stopped what I was doing and turned to look at her. The gimp was standing behind her with his leash intact, his head bowed and hands clasped in front of him.

"You socialise with the gimp outside of this environment? Do I know him?" I asked, now looking at the gimp a little closer.

"Does anyone ever know anyone, Talia? Most people do not know themselves."

I smiled at this, nodded my head and continued lining up my next shot.

"He is yours now," Lena said as she stepped back to present the gimp.

"Lena, I only agreed to take photos. I have no desire to participate. No offence, Mr Gimp. It's a lovely offer. This is just not who I am."

I shook my head at the idea and once again turned to focus on my work. A few minutes later, while I was in the process of changing the lighting, I realised the gimp was still standing in the doorway. Lena was nowhere to be seen.

"Really?" I said to the gimp, knowing that he would not respond. I let out a sigh and resigned myself to the fact that I now had a gimp.

"Come over here and change the lighting for me when I tell you."

He scurried across and stood at the lights, awaiting direction. Thus we became a wayward team of sorts. The gimp helped me set up lighting, he changed people's positions, altered the backdrops.

I left photographing Mistress le Vour and the gimp until last. There was a distance in his eyes that I could not place a measure on. It made it challenging to find a way to represent him in any particular light that would honour him. I understood that he played the role of a submissive, he wanted to be objectified and demeaned and that was the part that Mistress le Vour executed very well. I had never witnessed any sexual interaction between them. He was commanded and at times beaten. That was all I could see.

Jean Paul and the others missed me socially. I had been so consumed with the process that my nights were expended taking images and my days were filled with processing the film and developing the images. I no longer allowed anyone into the darkroom. I wanted this creative space to be untainted. Not even Lena was to see the results of my work until it was done and ready for exhibition.

Lena arranged for the picture frames to be custom-made by a local woodworker friend of hers. I wanted the frames to be thick, revealing the grain and colours of the wood, emphasising that there is beauty in allowing what is natural to be exposed, knots and all. The gallery space that she allocated for the exhibition was large with stark white walls. I worked with the gallery owner Andre and his assistant Zoran to place the images on the wall and adjust the lighting for maximum impact. The end result was spectacular; it had exceeded even my expectations.

The date was set for the exhibition. Lena had advertised in all the couture magazines. She had so many connections that she successfully stimulated intrigue in the art world. This opening night was going to be big. The night before the exhibition I allowed Lena to walk through the gallery. I waited outside, chain-smoking cigarettes while she laid eyes upon my work for the first time.

I hadn't realised until she walked into the room that I was nervous. I wanted her to like what I had produced and hoped that she understood that what I had created was my interpretation of what I had seen and experienced.

An hour later, she emerged from the gallery, her arms spread open for me to give her a cuddle as she said, "Dis is spectacular."

I let out a breath.

"Come, we must celebrate."

She grabbed my hand and we headed towards the Moulin Rouge.

***

That night the crew was together once more. I no longer felt sorry for Enzo and his submissive ways. I respected his choice to be the way he wanted to be and, more to the point, for being fearless about doing what he chose in public. I saw now that he was to be admired rather than pitied.

***

The exhibition opened the next day. We were all dressed up for the occasion. Lena had insisted I use her stylist to ensure I was all dolled up for the event. I took a deep breath as the car arrived at the gallery. They had a red carpet rolled out along the ground and photographers were taking images of the people arriving.

This was truly out of control.

When I entered the doorway, Jean Paul was waiting for me. He smiled, held out his arm for me to take it. I gladly accepted and walked forward. It was really crowded. The air was filled with the banter of people talking and pointing at the images on the walls. Lena had made arrangements for the waiters to be scantily dressed in leather bondage outfits. As a surprise, she had also hired the street saxophone-player that I liked. I loved it.

As I've said, the exhibition consisted of ten images arranged in various configurations for each subject. Instead of limiting myself to photography, I had introduced the technique of paper tole to parts of the images to emphasise depth and my interpretation of important aspects contained within them.

I had also placed random text on the walls to evoke what I wanted the viewer to see rather than have them looking through their own eyes. In essence, I didn't trust that the viewers could see past their own judgement and fears. This was my way of attempting to protect what I had captured. The words I used were: Fearless, Trust, Empathy, Lust, Pain, Love, Visceral, Power, Control, Strength, Purity, Truth.

I refused to do a speech; this had never been part of the deal.

Naturally, Lena stepped in and stole the show with her vivacious presence. She was already known so it worked for her to take the limelight. I was just pleased that I had completed this mammoth task with a feeling of self-satisfaction. I was proud of what I had achieved.

The exhibition was a total success with all the works sold. The terms of the sale were that the negatives would be destroyed so that the works were one of a kind. The only series that I didn't place for sale were the images I took of the gimp.

The whole of Paris seemed to be talking about the exhibition. Lena was becoming a celebrity now, making appearances as Madam le Vour. She was in her element.

On my last night in Paris, I went out with the crew

to party. I had been there for almost four months. The end of the exhibition signified the right time for me to move on. Lena had given me 50,000 euro as my share of the sales. It boggled my mind that people were willing to pay such large amounts of money for photos. Jean Paul explained that most of the buyers were the people I had photographed. Many influential clientele utilised Lena's services.

It made sense.

I used a portion of my newly acquired earnings to shout them an opulent evening of celebration.

***

The next day I packed my essentials into a suitcase and handed the keys to the loft back to the person I had rented it from. Jean Paul met me at the Lena's studio, as I had asked. Lena had left a note to say goodbye. I guess she wasn't prepared to risk being emotional. I could respect that. I drew a smiley face on her note to acknowledge her goodbye and left it there on her work stool.

Jean Paul broke the silence. "Do you have to go?"

I looked at him standing there with his head down and hands clasped in front of him. I smiled and said, "I do." He didn't shift so I walked towards him. "I asked you here, Jean Paul, because I have something for you." He raised his head and looked at me as I placed the stacked images of the gimp in front of him. "I believe these belong to you," I said with a smile.

The expression on his face changed to surprise. "You know?"

I nodded. "Only after you became my gimp assistant.

I noticed little things, like your ability to set up the lighting, the way you positioned people for me. I could see that you understood what I was trying to capture."

He looked down again as if sad that he had failed to maintain his anonymity.

I reached across and lifted his head so that his eyes were locked onto mine. "I'm giving you this series to honour your choice to be who you want to be. I also want you to have all my darkroom equipment, studio lighting. It's all yours. I'm not taking it with me."

In a small voice, shaking his head, he said, "This is not what I want."

Compassion flowed through me. "Jean Paul, I understand now when we met that you intentionally introduced me to Lena. I get that it was probably you who stimulated the opportunity for me to go behind that door and be introduced to another world. I voluntarily lived in that space for months. I don't feel uncomfortable there; I just don't have a desire to exist within those rules. It's not who I am."

He whispered, "I want to serve you."

I put my arms around him and whispered, "I would only want to set you free. Serve another if you feel you must. It cannot be me."

***

My last stop before I headed to the airport was my favourite café. I had a few hours before I needed to board my flight. I smoked the last of my cigarettes while sipping a glass of wine and listening to the street performer play that saxophone as though he was making love to the music he produced. There was something so haunting in the way he made that sound. He massaged the instrument with his fingers, his eyes were closed and his body would move to the execution of the notes. I flagged a taxi and signalled for him to wait a moment. I walked across to the busker and placed an envelope in his saxophone case. Then I climbed into the taxi and headed to the airport. I would miss him most of all.

Synchronicity

I arrived in Hungary to find Marton waiting to pick me up. It had been months since I had spoken with him so I was keen to find out how things were progressing on my grandparents' place. We spent a couple of nights in Budapest to give me an opportunity to chill. It was actually really nice to see him. He seemed happier than when we had first met. I assumed that came with familiarity. He was now becoming a friend rather than a person that I had hired.

We drove out to the manor, where my grandparents greeted me with open arms. It was lovely to see them. The first point of order was to eat. Everything seemed to involve food when I was with them. My grandmother had been cooking all day in preparation for my arrival so the house was infused with garlic and paprika.

The place had been transformed.

The gardens were now in bloom with beautiful displays of flowers. It felt as though I was visiting a fairyland. The inside of the house seemed brighter. They had been painting the rooms in lighter colours. The weathered wallpaper had been removed. So many simple alterations gave this place a welcome facelift. It was truly nice to be here.

Marton helped me arrange to hire a horse to ride from a man in the neighbouring village. It was a beautiful grey percheron mare that I nicknamed Tilly because I could not pronounce her real name. She had a beautiful length of stride when she trotted. It was wonderful to be back on a horse. There was something amazing about exploring the countryside on the back of a majestic beast. I had forgotten how grounded I felt around them.

I quickly found myself in a routine where I would wake in the morning, have breakfast with my grandparents and Marton, and then head off on horseback with a packed lunch to explore the forests that surrounded the area. I took a lot of landscape and nature images. I loved the texture of the bark on the birch trees in the forest. I had not yet managed to take any good images of the wildlife. My lenses were not suitable but that didn't stop me from trying. In this space I could appreciate that there were three key things that I needed to incorporate in my life with regularity: horses, travel and photography. I felt certain that these formed my basis for entertainment, stimulus, creativity and balance.

On my way back from a day trip I came across a horse-drawn caravan that had lost a wheel. I approached the people to ask if I could assist. They didn't speak any English and appeared to be cautious as I approached them. I decided to fetch Marton to translate and ask my grandfather to bring some equipment to help them.

Upon our return, they were still sitting around with the wheel off. The horses had been released to graze and they looked as though they were setting up camp.

"Talia, these people are gypsies," said Marton as we approached the camp.

"So, what does that mean?" I asked, wondering why that would matter.

"Gypsies tend to be thieves and liars. This is dangerous. We need to stay away from them."

I looked at him, annoyed. I couldn't believe my ears. In a scolding tone, I said, "What a load of rubbish. These people need help and I want us to help them."

Even my grandfather seemed hesitant to assist them.

I ignored them both and approached the gypsy caravan with my hands in the air, saying, "We want to help you fix this."

Marton translated.

The men stood and looked at me with an expression of warning.

"Please let us help you fix this," I said, again pointing to the wheel.

Marton once again translated.

I started moving the wheel towards the wagon. It was heavier than it looked. As I attempted to lift it and then to roll it, a man left the huddle and came to assist. I nodded my head, acknowledging his efforts, and leant the wheel against the wagon.

My grandfather took out his tools to start the repairs on the axle. It didn't take long before all the men were in a huddle exchanging thoughts on the best way to fix the problem.

***

After a few hours of tinkering and a lot of manpower, the wheel was back on as good as new. My grandpa and I stayed to accept a drink as their gesture to thank us. I asked Marton to head home and return with some of the multitude of leftovers that Grandma had. She was forever cooking up a storm, as if she expected an army of men to drop by.

When he returned, Grandma was with him. They unloaded the food and we sat around sharing a meal with the Romany gypsies. They told stories of their travels and it sounded like a romantic way to live. Nothing seemed to bind them to any place. They told us the folklore of tree spirits and nymphs as though it was real to them. I guess in a sense it was, because they believed it.

One of the older ladies, who had not spoken a word, wandered across to sit next to me. She said something as she reached out for my hand.

I looked at Marton.

"She wants to read your future," he explained.

I looked at her staring at my palm. She didn't say anything at first. She looked at my other hand and then went back to the first one again. Marton translated her words as she spoke.

"I'm sorry you have lost your parents so young." She had my attention. "Many men will try to love you but you will not love them back. What you want exists. He looks for you."

An image of Brad came into my mind.

But I had lost him.

She shook her head. "No," she said with such surety. "Help him." I nodded my head to acknowledge her words. "When you are ready, seek the man that is seeking you." Silently she continued to assess my palm. "Your life is blessed. You are protected by powerful magic. The one that helps you, she loves you like a daughter." Her face contorted as she rubbed a section of my palm as if to remove a smudge. "You are not cursed." Raising her weary eyes to greet mine, she extended her weathered hand to rest on my cheek.

I smiled.

"You are not cursed," she repeated.

My stomach sank. There was a truth to her words that even I couldn't deny. I felt as though I was like water, moulding to my surrounds and adapting, whereas the people who tried to follow me were like rocks that shattered when they hit an impasse.

I thanked her for the reading and we said our goodbyes to head back home.

***

The next day when I went out for my ride, they were gone. It felt like a dream. I couldn't get the words she had said out of my head. I would seek the man that seeks me. If it wasn't Brad, then who? I knew when she said that Brad needed my help that she was right. He had crept into my thoughts ever since I had arrived. I decided that night was to be my last in Europe. I needed to head back to Australia to put my mind at ease. If I called him he would pretend all was well. I knew there was truth to what the old woman was saying. Brad needed me.

***

The plane trip back to Australia was a smooth flight but the length of time it took sucked balls. I was never inclined to sleep on flights so it felt as though it was not going to end. When I arrived at Shane and Ruth's, no-one was home. This was unusual for them. I found the spare key and let myself in. As I looked around, I noticed some unopened mail on the kitchen table and a hand-written note: Alfred Hospital Maternity Ward Room 613.

I called Ruth.

"Hello."

"Hi, Ruth. It's Talia."

"How are you?" she said in an uplifting voice.

"I'm good. Is everything alright?"

"Suzanna is in hospital. She's been struggling to carry the baby to term. They hospitalised her the day before yesterday to see if they can stabilise her. It's too early to deliver."

"How's Brad holding up?"

"He's a mess. He could really use a friend right now."

"How are you and Shane holding up?"

"We're okay. Just trying to be supportive. It's frustrating as there's not much we can do except wait. When are we going to see you?"

"I'll do my best to make it sooner rather than later," I said, not wanting to let them know I was in country. "I'm going to call Brad. We'll chat soon, okay?"

"Okay, Talia. Bye." Her voice was strained, holding back the tears.

This was their first grandchild. Given that Ruth had struggled to conceive and loved being a mum, I could only imagine the amount of stress she was embracing around this ordeal. I don't know why, but I didn't want her to know I was in country. I needed to be present without expectation. I wasn't sure what I could do to assist, but perhaps by being supportive I would be contributing in some way.

I arrived at the prenatal ward in the Alfred Hospital and entered Room 613. Suzanna was in the bed sleeping and Brad was in a chair beside her with his head resting on her hand.

"Hey, Brad," I whispered in an attempt not to disturb Suzanna.

He raised his head, looked across at me and lit up.

"What're you doing here?" he said as he walked across and wrapped his arms around me.

"I'm not sure you would believe me if I told you," I said.

"Did Ruth call you?" he questioned.

"Nope," I said, smirking.

Assessing my expression, he guessed, "Were you already in town and didn't tell anyone?"

I stepped back and swayed from side to side as I said, "Nope, try again. You won't guess this in a million years."

He smiled as he stepped in to threaten to tickle me. "Well, tell me then."

"In the forests of Hungary, an old Romany gypsy told me I should help you. Here I am, at your service."

He had his arms folded, admiring me. "You never cease to surprise me, Talia."

"Hello," said a little voice.

I looked across at Suzanna, who was now trying to sit up.

"Let me help you." I adjusted her pillows so that they supported her better. "Hi, Suzanna. I'm Talia. I guess we've not really met properly yet." I gently touched her hand.

"Brad talks about you all the time so I kind of feel as though we have met," she said as she lay with her eyes closed.

Brad shrugged and I shook my head at the plethora of things he might have said to her.

"How are you feeling?" I asked.

"Okay, I guess. I'm a bit scared and really tired." Her voice was barely audible.

"Is there anything you need that I could get for you?"

"No, I think I might try and sleep some more."

"Sure, I'll head off to let you rest."

She opened her eyes to look at me and smiled. In a light voice, she made an unexpected request. "Actually, can you stay?"

I looked at her. *Was she talking to Brad or me?*

"I want you to stay, Talia, if that's okay," she confirmed.

"Sure, I can do that for you."

Suzanna smiled and closed her eyes.

Brad looked across at me, beaming, "I'm so happy that you're here, Talia."

I laughed. "Yeah, well you look like shit. Why don't you go and get some rest and I'll stay with Suzanna for a while. We can take shifts."

He looked across at her in the bed and hesitated. "Are you sure?"

I opened the door. "Absolutely. Go."

As he walked past, I smirked and said, "A little attention to some hygiene principles wouldn't go astray either." I laughed as I shut the door before he could comment.

I walked over to the chair that he had been sitting on and watched Suzanna in silence. The monitors that she was hooked up to indicated that she was stable. Her breathing was a bit laboured but I assumed that was part of pregnancy. I kept watch while she slept.

***

I had been in there for a little over two hours before Ruth and Shane came in. I signalled that I would meet them outside so Suzanna could maintain her slumber.

"Brad told me. I couldn't believe it. Why didn't you tell me you were here?" she said while hugging me. Without waiting for a response, she launched into her next question. "Is it true that you came here because a gypsy told you to?"

I laughed. "Actually, yes, that's true."

She stood back to inspect me.

"We're so happy to see you, Talia," said Shane, stepping in to give me a cuddle.

I squeezed him tight and said, "Thanks, Shane. Good to see you guys too."

I was conscious that Suzanna was in the room alone. "I should probably get back in there. I don't think that Suzanna wants to be left alone right now."

Ruth smiled as she touched my face. I think she was relieved that I cared about Suzanna's welfare. "That's okay. We're going to take over for a while. Here are the keys to the house we're staying at. Brad has already organised a room for you. Get over there and get some rest. We'll join you later."

They walked into the room.

***

I headed off to house, loving the idea of a hot shower and a warm bed. It was an old double-fronted Victorian. It was fully renovated and was leased out to families who needed to stay close to the hospital. When I walked inside, Brad was sitting at the kitchen table.

"Your room is on the secnd floor, first left. I placed you right next door to mine." He winked.

"How are you?" I said, standing in the doorway looking directly at him.

"I'm good," he responded, fingering the rim of his coffee cup.

I walked across, pulled out a chair and placed it in front of him. I sat in it and once again looked directly at him. "How are you?"

He paused his play with the cup and said, "I'm scared."

"What are you scared of?" I persisted, knowing he needed to release his fears.

"What if she …?"

I placed my hand on his arm. "Finish the sentence. What if she …?"

He looked at me. "Talia, I don't want to think about it."

I nodded. "You already are. It's swilling around in that brain of yours. Face your fears. What if she …?"

He looked at me, took a deep breath and said, "What if she dies? I could never forgive myself. She's carrying my baby. This is all happening because of me."

I squeezed his arm. "She won't die," I said calmly.

"You don't know that. You can't say that for sure. Talia, I love her; I am in love with her. I cannot lose her."

I pulled him into my arms. "She will live. Your baby will live and you will all have a wonderful life together. I promise."

His head was leaning on my shoulder as he spoke. "When I got back from Europe, I resented her for being pregnant. I sometimes even wished that she would miscarry." He sobbed deeply.

"None of that matters. Let it go. What's happening now is not your fault. Shhhh." I rocked him in my arms as I would a child.

He was in so much pain, feeling guilt for his past

thoughts. He needed to release the past and embrace the present. That was all that mattered.

When Brad settled down, I suggested he get some rest and I would do the same. I wanted to speak to the doctors to understand exactly what was happening. I needed to know what the options were. I may not have been in a position to fix what was happening, but I could ensure that she and her unborn child received the best attention and access to the best facilities available. I wanted to do anything I could to ensure that Brad had his chance at 'happily ever after'.

***

The doctors confirmed that Suzanna needed to stay on bed rest to prevent her from going into early labour. The risk was that the baby's lungs had not yet fully matured so the best option was to keep her immobile to allow the baby a chance to develop in the womb. It was estimated that another two to three weeks would be required.

I spent the evenings and most of the night with Suzanna and then the rest of the family took it in turns to watch over her during the day while I slept. At night I told her stories about my experiences travelling abroad. I read her excerpts from books she nominated and for the most part she would keep still and listen.

Three weeks and two days later she went into labour and gave birth to a beautiful healthy little baby. We were all waiting for the announcement when Brad came out of the theatre.

"It's a girl, a healthy little girl!"

We all smothered him in hugs. It had been an exhausting time with a welcome outcome.

Ruth yelled out, "I'm a grandma," as she jumped in the air.

Shane hugged her as he cried tears of joy and relief. It was exhilarating to know that both mother and baby were well.

Suzanna was taken back to her room and the baby was placed in a crib to be monitored while she rested. They all gooed and gaaed at the tiny baby through the glass. She looked perfect, as all babies do when they are only a minute old. Brad beamed with pride. I soaked up his radiance and loved knowing that he was a father.

"Have you picked out a name for her yet?" I asked.

He turned his head to look at me. "Mia Talia Parker."

I glanced at Brad and then back at the baby then across at Brad again.

"It was Suzanna's idea. She insisted," he said reassuringly.

I didn't know what to say. I looked across at Mia in the crib. "She's a very lucky little girl."

"She's my princess," he said as he placed his hand on the glass.

I was feeling a little overwhelmed and exhaustion was getting the better of me. "I'm going to head back and take a shower. It's been a long day."

Brad didn't divert his gaze from his baby girl as he responded with, "Okay."

***

After my rest, I returned. Mia had been moved into the room with Suzanna. When I entered, Brad was holding Mia in his arms and Suzanna was sitting up, smiling.

"Congratulations, Mum," I said as I leaned in and gave her a kiss on the cheek.

"Isn't she beautiful?" she said, beaming.

"Absolutely! She's gorgeous. She clearly takes after you," I said, laughing.

Brad stuck out his tongue. "Sticks and stones."

Suzanna tapped Brad's arm. "Would you like to hold her, Talia?"

I stepped back, waving my hands. "No, I'm good."

Mia was eminently breakable and I had never held a child before. I didn't want this to be my first time.

"You're scared to hold a baby?" said Brad teasingly as he closed in.

"How long do you have to stay in here, Suzanna?" I asked in an attempt to ignore Brad.

"The doctor said we could go home as soon as tomorrow."

"That's awesome news. I'm glad."

I watched Brad making faces at Mia and rocking her in his arms. He looked so happy.

"I'm going to head off so I wanted to say goodbye. Congratulations to you both. I'm relieved that everything worked out."

Brad looked up. "Where are you going? You're not leaving again?"

I smiled. "Yes."

Suzanna looked across at Brad. "Honey, can you give Talia and I a minute? I want to speak to her alone."

He hesitated and then walked out with Mia. I stepped in to be closer to Suzanna and I looked at her face beaming up at me with an angelic smile.

"Thank you," she said.

I returned her gaze and remained silent.

"I will always be grateful to you for allowing me to love him."

I shook my head. "He chose you, Suzanna. He's here because he wants to be. It has nothing to do with me."

Tears welled in her eyes. "No, he chose obligation and I was okay with that. I believed that I had enough love for both of us. It was only when faced with this recent crisis that I saw him look upon me as I had seen him look at you. I realised that he finally loved me too."

I nodded my head. "I can see that too."

She paused for a moment to look at my hand on her arm. "I am never going to be what you are to him. I accept that. I'm happy to embrace the love that we have for one another because it's more than enough for me. Brad needs you in his life. I see that now." She paused, looked up into my eyes and said, "I even feel that I need you too."

She placed her hand on mine. "I know that you feel you need to go. I'm not trying to stop you. I just want you to know that we want you in our lives. You are family to us. You are family to me."

I nodded, knowing that if I didn't leave soon I would probably start shedding a tear. She didn't hate me. She wanted to embrace me and accept me for who I was to Brad and now to her. That was a very forgiving and bold move on her part.

"It was nice to finally meet you, Suzanna. Brad chose well." I squeezed her hand and then walked out of the room, closing the door behind me.

As I reached the exit, the automatic doors opened and a cool breeze greeted me. I welcomed the crisp air, as I found the hospital environment stifling. In the background, the sound of a person running grew louder.

"Talia!" yelled Brad. "You weren't planning to leave without saying goodbye, were you?"

I placed my arms around him and gave a big squeeze. "You're already an awesome dad."

He broke the hug and looked at me. "Am I going to see you again?" he said with a concerned look across his brow.

"Of course, I promise."

With this, he placed me in his arms and hugged the wind out of me.

"Don't run away from me. I want you in my life, always."

I closed my eyes and said, "And you in mine, always."

He watched me walk down the road. I hailed a passing cab, directing the driver to head towards the city. I didn't look back; I only wanted to look forward. This chapter of my past had to end here. I was relieved that everything was fine but felt drained.

The taxi driver dropped me off at Brunswick Street, Fitzroy. I had no idea what my next steps were. Fate would need to lead the way. I ordered a coffee and sat outside to allow the breeze to carry away my exhaustion and sorrow. The dulcet tones of wind chimes hanging outside a musty old second-hand bookstore called to me.

I walked in and gravitated to a specific book on a shelf. I pulled it out, closed my eyes and opened to a page. My fingers landed on a passage.

If it feels so good loving the wrong person, imagine how wonderful it is going to be when you love the right one.

I took a deep breath and closed the book, placing it back where it had been.

As I turned to walk out the door, the man behind the counter peered through the top of his bifocals. "Did you get the message you needed to receive?"

I smiled thoughtfully. "Yes, I believe I did." And then I walked out the door.

It was uncanny to receive such an apt message when I felt completely lost for direction. I had experienced enough in my life to appreciate that all things happened for a reason. This was a clear sign. Perhaps it was time for me to consider being brave enough to seek out the one that was seeking me. Brad had showed me it was possible; now it was time for me to believe.

Lightning Source UK Ltd.
Milton Keynes UK
UKOW05f2211290115

245376UK00015B/277/P